CW00822408

Whisper in the Reeds

M. Desmond McConnell

Whisper in the Reeds

Olympia Publishers
London

www.olympiapublishers.com
OLYMPIA PAPERBACK EDITION

A CIP catalogue record for this title is
available from the British Library.

ISBN: 978-1-78830-440-5

This is a work of fiction.
Names, characters, places and incidents originate from the writer's
imagination. Any resemblance to actual persons, living or dead, is
purely coincidental.

First Published in 2022

Olympia Publishers
Tallis House
2 Tallis Street
London
EC4Y 0AB
Printed in Great Britain

Dedication

For my loving parents, Myra and Desmond McConnell. To my patient wife, Kristina, and our amazing daughters, Ava and Mya — without whom, this story would never have seen the printed page. My deepest appreciation goes to Heather Weeks and Leslie Palermo for their thoughtful edits and feedback.

Acknowledgements

Thanks to Penny Bonsal's *Irish RMs*, from which I was able to glean valuable historical information pertaining to the life of my great-grandfather, John Charles Milling, RM, and his most callous assassination.

Milling, John Charles - Royal Irish Constabulary Officers: A
biographical dictionary and genealogical guide 1816-1922' by Jim
Herlihy, Four Courts Press 2004.

Prologue

Resident magistrates, or RMs, found their roots in the 1830s as the British government responded to the perceived inadequacies of Irish county Justices of the Peace. Irish RMs were appointed by the British government in an effort to curb the corruption and inefficiency of the Irish magistracy at the time. Justices of the peace were expected to be men of adequate social standing to build the respect from their neighbours and the community at large. As a result, resident magistrates were pulled from the landed gentry in the United Kingdom to serve as administrators and enforcers of the law. On rare occasions, the Crown recruited RMs from the RIC (Royal Irish Constabulary), as was the case in the mysterious events surrounding the murder of the Right Honourable John Charles Milling, RM.

Irish RMs appointed by the British government were brought into an area from outside to fulfil the role of a local magistrate and to act as a guide and advisor to other lay magistrates. The RMs were considered loyal to the Crown and in effect became easy targets for the growing Nationalist sentiment and public unrest opposing British rule in Northern Ireland at the turn of the twentieth century.

The Royal Irish Constabulary (RIC) policed Northern Ireland until 1922. Some eighty-five thousand men served in the RIC between 1918 and 1922, with about eighty percent being Irish Catholics. In 1922, the RIC was disbanded and replaced by two police forces, the Garda Síochána (Guardians of the Peace) who policed the Irish Free State (now the Republic of Ireland), and the Royal Ulster Constabulary (RUC) who patrolled Northern Ireland (part of the United Kingdom). At its pinnacle, the RUC had approximately eight thousand five hundred officers, with an additional four thousand five hundred who were reservists. During the troubles in Ireland, three hundred members of the RUC were killed and a further nine thousand were injured in paramilitary-style attacks, mostly by the Provisional IRA. In the early eighties, the RUC carried the stigma of being the deadliest police force in the world.

The author has employed some poetic licence with the events in this tale; however, at the heart of this narrative is the assassination of John Charles Milling, RM (1873–1919), and the subsequent fictional account is interspersed with some historically accurate events and characters. Other sundry historical figures have been added to lend to the historical authenticity. The representation of any and all historical figures is purely fictional (with the exception of the assassination of John Charles Milling) and by no means intends to cast any aspersions or judgement upon those individuals. Any implications as to the guilt or innocence of any person mentioned in this tale are purely coincidental.

The author would like to thank Penny Bonsall for her extensive historical research and details about the life of the Honourable John Charles Milling, culminating in the publication of 'The Irish RMs: The Resident Magistrates in the British Administration in Ireland', published by Four Courts Press.

Chapter One
John C. Milling, RM

"Ya reddy?" a harsh brogue tongue whispered to another soot-blackened face hidden among the reeds, as the yellow-orange orb languidly succumbed to the horizon.

"Ya, Joe! Let's git dis ov'r widt! Ma misses wil' be wond'ring were I ham."

The barrel of the Enfield crept slowly from the reeds hugging the lush western Irish coastline. Lonesome seagulls drifted lazily above cresting waves breaking on the late evening, sun-speckled, glistening sand. Another glorious finale to a fine Westport spring day. A calloused labourer's hands fumbled momentarily with a single .303 cartridge as he placed it methodically into the chamber. Several hundred yards away a black Model A trundled eagerly down the grassy lane and pulled up to an ornately decorated Victorian house. The last rays of sunshine filtered off the eaves of the house and onto two weathered faces hidden deep among the reeds. The bolt-action sound cut through the squawk of gulls gathered overhead; those keen, scavenger eyes skimmed the surface of the shoreline.

"Ahhh... don't ya wurry aboot ya misses, Joseph MacBride, she'll be long goone now under da auspices of da whisky."

"Auspices? Ya bin readin' da dictionary agan, Joseph?"

"Shut the fook up, ya feckin eejit! Und pay attention to da hous'!"

The door of the Model A creaked slowly open, and a pair of shiny black shoes exited.

"Daddah! Daddah's home, Ma! Daddah's home!" Little Maggie Milling ran as fast as her little feet could carry her over to the window of the old Victorian. She began to wave feverishly at her father. Mr. John Charles Milling responded in like while removing his briefcase from the car as he started up toward the house. He sniffed the air quizzically, eye glasses perched neatly upon his nose, but his thoughts diverted as little Maggie stood bobbing excitedly on the front steps awaiting his arrival.

"Maggie, dearest, hav' ya bin waitin' 'ere all dayh?"

John Charles Milling was born March 27th, 1873 at Glasson, near Althlone, County Westmeath, the second son in the tradition of service in the constabulary. His grandfather, Oliver Milling, had served as a parish constable in Ardee, County Louth, and ended his career as RIC County Inspector in Tyrone from 1873 to 1877. While stationed at Kilfinane in County Limerick, Oliver Milling led a force of constabulary that lifted the siege of Kilmallock police barracks in the abortive Fenian rising[1] of 1867. John Charles Milling's father, also named Oliver Milling, served in many parts of Ireland during his years in the RIC and was finally appointed County Inspector in 1887 for West Mayo.

John Charles was no less distinguished. He was a popular officer among his colleagues and well-liked by his superiors.

Having gained three favourable records from the riots in July of 1909, John C. Milling was well on his way to a bright and favourable future in law enforcement. One account of Milling's steadfast bravery during the early riots recounted:

"as the rioting mob advanced towards DI Milling and his officers a barrage of stones hit them from which several officers were injured, including DI Milling, who received a serious leg wound. However, Milling and his men neatly caught the perpetrators and disbanded the riots."

After this incident, Detective Inspector Milling was transferred to Glenravel barracks in the summer of 1910. In 1912 Milling received yet another merit of distinction in the aftermath of another troubled summer in Belfast. It was a time of much civil unrest in Northern Ireland, with growing nationalist sentiment and opposition to the Home Rule Bill[2] imposed by the Crown. Such was the gravity of the situation that troops were stationed nearby in Mullingar to move at a moment's notice to Belfast when needed.

Chapter Two
Detective Inspector Scott

"Inspector! Inspector! O'er 'ere. Looks like we've foun' som'sing!"

Detective Inspector Scott may be described as an austere man in his mid-forties with grey whiskers bristling from a strong jawline. His athletic appearance and broad, powerful shoulders matched a permanent scowl characteristic of the Plymouth brethren[1]. In his right hand, he was never seen without his distinctive cherry wood calabash pipe. Scott moved steadily towards the sergeant, wading through the tall grasses and reeds, then stopping abruptly in his tracks. As DI Scott appeared over the hill, he studied the shoreline and the broken patch of reeds beneath him.

The Scott family also had a lengthy tradition of sons entering the Royal Irish Constabulary. Detective Inspector William Scott had been with the force since his early twenties and had undergone basic training alongside John Charles Milling at the Phoenix Park Training Depot[2]. For the Scott men, there was never any question of any other vocation, either in his mind or that of his family. "Ya never break with tradition…" were the resounding words of his father and grandfather that were firmly entrenched in Scott's psyche.

"Lads o're dare!" DI Scott pointed to a small patch of

spent cartridges to the left of a large imprint of a body in broken reeds.

"So, we've got more dhan one shot, lads! And it only took one shot to bring down the Honourable Mister Milling! Our witnesses say only one shot was fired," DI Scott continued. "So, find me dah udders fast, fellahs! We'r gunna fend this killa, dare's no question aboot it! John Milling was a highly respected member of dis community und a personal friend... I shall not rest until dis scum is found — dead or alive! It doesn't mutta eddah to me an unch!"

A squad car pulled up and three constables exited and strode purposefully towards DI Scott. The two shorter and smaller constables followed a stout and heavily-set, balding constable in his mid-thirties. McHugh, or 'Q' as his fellow officers called him, moved awkwardly, waddling through the tall reeds and shuffling like a penguin. McHugh looked perturbed at expending any energy greater than a sloth. Walking through the sand was hard work for a lethargic, slightly out-of-shape officer such as Q. His Webley revolver was perched upon his hip in true RIC fashion. Q carried the rank of sergeant and spent his time behind the front desk at the local branch of the RIC, and the remainder of his time at the local pub. He opened and closed the Westport police station and frequently cleaned broken glass at the station in the aftermath of cowardly attacks after hours by the Sinn Fein[3] youth, or those *"fookin' thugs who need a boot up their urse"* as Q liked to say. In fact, among Q's other talents lay the ability to coin a certain memorable phrase.

DI Scott stoically leant over the pile of spent cartridges nestled among the broken reeds. He picked one up and sniffed it like he was trying to assess its bouquet, as if it were a finely aged Merlot from Tuscany blended with a Sangiovese.

"Hmmmm. Dare woz a time I could tell which gunsmith produced da powdah… but alas no more." Scott shuffled uneasily on his feet, then stood motionless, his eyes fixated upon the Milling's home in the brief distance.

"Tis a grand vantage point 'ere, no question aboot it. Apparently, our perpetrator or perpetrators knew dis shoreline very well." He scrutinized the land and shoreline before him, raising and tilting his head slightly to take in the scents travelling in the breeze.

"Q!" yelled Scott suddenly. In response, a bustling in the reeds preceded and the stout Irishman came rolling over the sand with his two constables neatly in tow.

"Yes, Inspector! Ya found som'sing?" puffed Q.

"Naaaah, nothing else…" Q looked even more put out. "But 'ave ya men scour dis area a mile each way up und duhne the beach for more evidence. Und git Hentschell und O'Brien to take a cast of doze footprints ov'r dare. It may cuhm in 'andy when da time cuhmes. I'm heading up to the Millings' home to pay my respects to da widah. Cuhm find me if ya turn up som'sing else okay, boys?" continued Scott.

DI Scott set forth at a steady pace over the sand and cut an impressionable swath through the reeds. His mind turned toward little Maggie Milling. "Poor lass!" he thought. "Woteva will become of a widah und her child in deese tuff times."

Three solemn knocks rang out through the old Milling Victorian. Scott could hear faint, muffled sobbing, coming from an upstairs window slightly ajar. DI Scott thought momentarily whether this was an appropriate time to proceed, but he was powerless to move. His feet turned to lead and appeared to be cemented to the stoop. He heard footsteps coming down the wooden hallway and he straightened his jacket and tie, cleared his throat and prepared for whatever may greet him. He contemplated, reaching deep for the right words. The door opened briskly and a slight, delicate woman in her late twenties, long flowing locks of red auburn hair, wearing an apron and flowered dress, stood gazing inconsolable into Scott's eyes, her red, teary puffy eyes beacons of abject desperation.

"Mrs. Milling, I'm sorry to bodah ya, but me und m' men woz in da vicinity und I want t' express m' deepest sympathy und regrets fur ya loss. As ya well know, Mrs. Milling, John woz a close friend of mine und he will be sorely missed by me, m' men und da 'hole community. 'Tis a very terrible day in Westport, indeed! Und I promise ya, I shall do everyt'ing in m' power to bring deeze thugs to justice!"

No sooner had the words come out, Mrs. Milling crumbled to her feet and DI Scott jumped in and delicately swept Lilla back to her feet. He always perceived Lilla as a small, fragile, porcelain-like doll, but she now seemed even more tenuous than ever. There was something DI Scott found warming to his heart about her vulnerability; something almost endearing. Under DI Scott's arms, Lilla appeared like a small prey caught under the wings of a giant hawk. Scott had lived next door to the Millings from the day they had moved into the old Victorian three years ago. The police and justices commanded a close-knit community, and it was not uncommon for law enforcement and particularly those of similar denomination in smaller towns and villages, to live as neighbours. This served a twofold purpose, allowing for easier and more efficient communications between colleagues, and building closer relationships between law enforcement officers and justices of the peace.

"Oh my!" Lilla whimpered. "Mustn't I look like a silly fool?"

"Ma'm, dare's nothin' foolish in mourning for a loved one." Scott helped her to the living room where Lilla sat down at a cherry wood dining table.

"What am I to do? Poor Maggie is beside herself. She woz awfully close to her fadha, ya know…"

DI Scott shuffled his feet again, something he tended to do when faced with agonizing social moments. He carried the reputation in the community of being a just and fine detective who knew his craft well, but when it came to the fairer sex in social settings, he was utterly inept.

"Ummm… well… do ya tink it'd help if I spoke widh' da liddle lass? Tell her how her fadha was well loved by dis 'hole community?" As the words left his mouth, Scott realized he really wasn't prepared for this. The poor girl had just lost her father, and what could he possibly say to lessen her grief?

"Tank you, DI Scott, but if I taught dhat wood help Maggie, I'd say yes, but she's just so distraught. She hasn't eaten a ting! And she's been in her room all dayh. Now she won't even cumhe out!"

"Ahhh well… tis best t' leave her alone fo' now, I tink. I'll be next door. If you need anything, call on me day or night; don't be afraid of waking me now, ya hear?"

"I shall keep ya in mind if anyting cumhes up, tank-you, Mr Scott." Lilla bid DI Scott farewell, thanking him for his support and friendship. The door closed tightly behind Lilla as her footsteps faded down the hallway. DI Scott perched upon the front stoop for a few pensive moments before moving forward. He considered how he might guide Lilla in applying for compensation through the courts. After all, her husband was killed in the line of duty as a resident magistrate. And how else would a widowed woman be able to support herself and her child?

The red brick façade of the police station sat across the street from the two-story town hall. DI Scott walked up the cobblestone path leading up to the station, smoking his calabash, and stopped momentarily to kick the sand from the soles of his shoes. As he entered the station house, he was greeted by Constable Hentschell seated squarely behind a large oak desk. Hentschell perused a stack of manila folders slapped haphazardly across the desk. The morning sunlight passed through the small windows to succinctly illuminate the room with a quiet, reassuring light.

"Is dhat tea I smell a-brewing, Hentschell?"

"Yes, sir, I just put a pot on," continued Hentschell. "Please 'elp yourself, Detective Inspector."

DI Scott walked over to the stove at the back of the office. He poured himself some tea in his customary Royal Dalton teacup, sipping the tea methodically as he started to hum a little upbeat ditty known as the Foxhunt. Hentschell looked quizzically over at Scott but turned his gaze back to the folders sprawled across his desk.

"This scoundrel, James Lynchehaun, looks like a possibility," declared Hentschell, interrupting the crescendo of Scott's tune.

"James Lynchehaun is nothin' more dhan a cowardly, woman-beating lout. I've had the dubious pleasure of meeting our Jimmy Lynchehaun und he doesn't 'ave the brains nor the wherewithal to pull off som'sing like dis…"

Scott slid over to the desk. "Naaahh, Lynchehaun is a pathetic animal with not enuff scruples or patience for dis crime, Hentschell. Lemme take a gander at doze udder files." Scott pulled up an old wooden stool beside Hentschell. Hentschell was a younger officer with only two years' experience in the force. Like all the officers under Scott's command, Hentschell deeply admired his mentor. Although Hentschell appeared to be a slender athletic young man with a muscular build, Scott towered over all his men, standing a little over seven foot three inches. DI Scott perched upon a dainty wooden stool that appeared to buckle under his weight as he flicked through the files on the desk.

"'ere look closely at deese, Hentschell… Deese two men I know equally well as our thug, Mr. Lynchehaun. The brothers MacBride! Yeah, deese two fellas look more promising alright…"

"Wot makes you so sure, sir?" Hentschell interjected, half-heartedly.

"Just tink of da scene of our crime! Dare woz evidence of two perpetrators at da scene, woz dare not?"

"Yes, dare woz, sir! And deese two men live in Westport too!" interjected Hentschell.

"Ahhh… yes indeed, Hentschell… And both deese men are known members of Sinn Fein. So, I tink our two brudahs may well git a visit from us today. Let's round up da boys und head out as soon as McHugh und da udders are done investigating da scene of da crime. Dhat'll give us som' time to look ov'r da rest of deese files."

Chapter Three
The MacBride's

Cattle manure hung oppressively low in the early evening air as the constables neared the outskirts of the MacBride farm. The farm ambled along a patchy, broken forest line of large oaks and beach trees dotted here and there, interspersed only by a partially standing ancient stone wall peppered by bitter-vetch and yellow archangel. Crowning the pastoral view in the distance sat the summit of Croagh Patrick[1] monumentally towering over the landscape, a mere ten kilometres southwest of the village.

Old Seamus MacBride, the youngest, Anthony, and his more infamous older brother, Major John MacBride[2], were born at The Quay in Westport. Their father, Patrick MacBride, had been a shopkeeper and trader up until his untimely death. John, the eldest, had the privilege of attending the Christian Brothers' School in Westport and later St. Malachy's College in Belfast. He served as major in the Irish Transvaal Brigade, fighting against the British in the Second Boer War[3] until its conclusion in 1902. After the Boer War, John had a brief interlude in Paris where he married the actress, Maud Gonne[4]. Their marriage failed after two years; around the time their son Sean was born. After their divorce, John returned to Dublin. Shortly thereafter, John joined the Irish Republican

Brotherhood — a secret oath-bound fraternal organization dedicated to the establishment of an independent democratic republic in Ireland founded in 1858 until 1924, when it faded into dust. A short time after he moved to Dublin, John started working for a chemist's firm. Through his colleagues at the firm, he learnt of the Celtic Literary Society, where he came to be a close acquaintance with Arthur Griffith[5]. After gaining Griffith's trust, John soon became embroiled in the Irish Republican fight, for which he eventually played a notable role in the Easter Rising of 1916[6] by happenstance. John was so well known by the British, that he had intentionally been removed from all strategic planning by the Irish Nationalist leaders to ensure as little counterintelligence made it back to the British about the upcoming rebellion. On the morning of Easter Monday, John was in Dublin planning to meet his brothers Seamus and Anthony. Both brothers recently arrived from Westport, since Anthony, a doctor, was in the city for his planned wedding on Wednesday of Easter week. As John left his brothers and walked up Grafton Street, he came upon Thomas MacDonagh[7] in uniform leading his troops to take their positions at Jacob's Biscuit Factory. John swiftly offered his services and was duly appointed second-in-command at Jacob's Biscuit Factory[8], where they fought and were ordered to eventually surrender to the British. They saw little action while entrenched at Jacob's Biscuit Factory, since British troops chose to remain in central Dublin. In the aftermath of the failed Easter Rising, both MacBride and MacDonagh were taken into custody at Kilmainham Goal and executed by the British on May 3rd and 5th, 1902, respectively. It's reported that MacDonagh whistled as he was being escorted from his cell to the waiting firing squad. While MacBride requested no blindfold, he purportedly announced to his executioners: *"I have looked down the muzzles of too many guns in the South African war to fear death and now please carry out your sentence."*

Perhaps humbled by his brother's experiences in war, Seamus chose to remain in Westport, where he married a local farmer's daughter and was given sixty acres of farmland by his father-in-law as a dowry. Rumours were that business hadn't been good for Seamus' father and the gifting of the farmland was less parental generosity and more necessity. Seamus and his wife had three sons, the first dying in childbirth, leaving only Joseph and Leigh, both of whom were known associates of the local chapter of the Irish Republican Brotherhood (IRB). Scott and his men had long had the MacBride brothers on their 'watch' list.

The serenity ended abruptly at the crunch of feet marching toward the old stone farmhouse half a mile away. The sun languidly crested upon the horizon as DI Scott and the other constables stopped in obedient formation as their leader lifted an enormous paw in the air. He motioned to his constables to drop quickly to the ground, which they did so precisely upon command. Their hands moved fast to their holstered revolvers in unison, expecting the worse. Scott peered through the brush and looked back at the line of constables crouching in his wake. Young Hentschell to his left looked resolute, as if accepting whatever fate brought their way. A black van carrying several men passed the constables hidden among the bushes.

The farmhouse stood several hundred feet away — east of a barn and solitary cattle shed. A ramshackle chicken coup built out of chicken wire and oddly cut pieces of worn lumber leant over to the left of the barn. A lone rooster pecked at the ground and strutted around a mass of perky hens. DI Scott and the constables leant forward, eyeing the farmhouse. A small fire flickered away inside seen through partially drawn paisley curtains. Shadows danced across the drab interior walls. Scott signalled the constables to remove their Webley's from their holsters. Their weapons drawn; the constables were ready to pounce at the slightest sign of alarm. The DI rose slowly and glanced quickly from barn to farmhouse. Hentschell appeared to move in unison with his leader, followed closely by the others as they advanced forward. The sound of a fox far in the distance was heard crying, a chilling and discomforting sound like that of a baby in painful distress.

The constables fanned out, nearing the farmhouse, as Scott motioned to Hentschell to stay close. The two men approached the front door with caution as the other constables moved to strategic predetermined points around the farm. Scott reached out his giant fist and knocked three times on the aged, weathered wooden door. Flecks of faded blue paint fell to the ground. The sound rang out in the crisp evening air like a hawk signalling its mate. Footsteps approached the door while muffled voices made terse, mumbled exchanges. Scott and Hentschell stood their ground with Webley's aimed. The door creaked open slowly and a frail, demur, grey-haired man in his late sixties stood alone in the doorway. Old man MacBride appeared uneasy as his cautious blue eyes scanned the two officers with weapons drawn.

"Gentl'men! We don't need nunhe of ya trouble 'ere! Ya cun put doze weapons away. Wot cun I do fur ya?"

"Mr. MacBride, we're 'ere to speak widh ya sons. Are dhey not home?"

"Aye, dhey're 'ome alright, but wot it is ya wanting widh dhem?"

"Sir, dhat's a matta fur da authorities und not fa ya t' wurry aboot!" continued Scott.

At that very moment two shots rang out from behind the farmhouse, as DI Scott and Hentschell rushed to the rear of the abode they were greeted by the two MacBride brothers lying face down in the mud. Old man McBride quickly hobbled after Scott and Hentschell, his severely bowed, rickets-riddled legs seeming to buckle under his weight.

"Don't shoot 'em! Don't shoot 'em!" Seamus could be heard yelling as he hobbled forward.

"Ahhh, Mr. MacBride, doncha ya wurry, m' men are not killahs. We just want t' speak widh ya boys, dhat's all."

"Dhey've done nothin' wrong! Why da ya hound 'em so?" squawked the pale old man.

"If dhey 'ave nothin' t' hide dhen why should dhey feel a need t' run?" piped Hentschell.

The two constables crouched with one knee firmly entrenched into the brothers' shoulder blades. They removed handcuffs from their belts and placed them around the brothers' wrists.

"Dare's no need fur dhat!" yelled old man MacBride. "Why are ya harassing m' boys so?"

"Mr. MacBride, we not 'ere to harass anyone! We merely want to speak with 'em," continued Scott. "If dhey 'ave nothin'

t' hide dhen ya shall see 'em agan t'morrah befor' sundown!"
A squad of constables hauled the two brothers away on foot
down the country lane towards town. Old man MacBride just
shook his head and stood watching as they moved away and
disappeared around the corner. All the while, the two brothers
were cursing, swearing and spitting at the constables
restraining them.

The Westport police station, formerly a thatched-roof
cottage, loomed innocuously set against its equally welcoming
counterparts on the prosperous Newport Road. Newport Road
ran from the centre of Westport village to the neighbouring
town of Newport about sixteen miles north. Sitting off the
main room of the police station to the east, was an old worn
oak desk and a smaller room commonly used for sundry
purposes such as interrogation and equipment storage. Now
the room stood spotless and empty with one solitary Regency
table and four rosewood caned chairs tucked neatly
underneath. DI Scott set the room up specifically for
interrogation when needed, but he was often found there late
at night pondering the various criminal cases and offences that
befell his jurisdiction, illuminated only by a single paraffin
lamp.

Scott recalled the multitude of times Milling had stopped
by the station to deliberate a certain case, a conundrum or a
specific person or persons in the community. He was a rare
individual who cared about the people in his town. This was
an uncommon trait in so many other justices of the peace and
RMs, particularly RMs who were appointed from outside of
Ireland, as they so commonly were. The Millings, as Plymouth
brethren, came from a nonconformist Evangelical Christian

sect with roots in Dublin dating back to the 1820s. Plymouth brethren had strong ties to the community with men having a long-standing tradition of law enforcement. But above and beyond enforcing the law, they were men who kept their word; men who didn't put principle before the human condition. They were men who recognized the elemental nature of humanity and the inequities that came with it. Through misfortune of birth and circumstances beyond their control, the majority did not live in an egalitarian world. Milling's words still rippled through Scott's head: "I hope dhat when I face m' creator, dhat m' actions und m' life are judged widh da same fairness fur which I hope I 'ave judged doze who 'ave com' b'fore me." Scott could see John's bright blue eyes illuminating the whole room as the words trickled off his golden tongue like treacle onto a moist chocolate cake.

Chapter Four
Interrogation

The grandfather clock in the police station chimed five in the evening as the officers escorted the MacBride brothers into the interrogation room. Q and Hentschell moved the two brothers into the barren room and directed them to be seated in chairs on opposite ends of the table. DI Scott followed closely behind, the room now a tad snug with five large men nestled together. The MacBride brothers noticeably averted their gaze from DI Scott — whom they both knew all too well from previous run-ins. Scott removed his calabash from his front coat pocket and started to methodically fill it with tobacco. He paused for a second, eyeing both men carefully sizing the two brothers up and determining who was the weakest.

"Ya know, I've bin smokin' dis pipe since I took da post of detective inspect'r 'ere in Wesport sum' tree years ago now." Scott paused for a second before continuing. "Und ya know wot?" He paused again before completing his train of thought. "I've learnt t' make a distinction between good tobacco und bad." There was a longer pause before Scott commenced once again. "...und dis tobacco smells awfully bad." Scott pursed his lips and stared suspiciously at the brothers. "List'n 'ere, boys! We don't want t' take up ya valuable time, or ours for dhat mattah. So, let's be sensible, shall we?"

The MacBride brothers both stared uneasily at each other from opposite ends of the table but knew better than to break their silence.

"'Ere's wot I propose, boys," declared Scott. "Ya tell us exactly wot kind of shenanigans you've bin up t' lately und ya'll both be outta 'ere before sunrise. Udderwise it's goin' t' be a long und arduous night for da both of ya."

Hentschell leaned forward and moved his hand to his truncheon just as Scott finished. This caught the attention of the two brothers.

"List'n!" shouted the older MacBride brother, Leigh. He slowly leaned forward as he spoke, resting his elbows on the table. "...we don't know nothin' aboot dis murdah! Tis the gawd's honest truth!"

"Und wot would the eidha of ya know aboot the gawd's honest truth, Mr. MacBride!? Dhat's da most comical ting I've heard all night lads!" continued Scott, as he turned, grinning at the constables. Hentschell knew the drill, he was wiser beyond his years, and keen to learn new tricks. He bade his time and waited for his cue from Scott before jumping in. Interrogation was a fine art, one they all learned well from DI Scott's tutorage. Hentschell could hear Scott's voice in his head... "Remember, lads, interrogation 'tis a fine art... give ya perpetrator just enough rope t' hang himself und dhen swoop in fur da kill. Ya hav' t' know when t' push und when t' loosen ya grip. Just like a tug o' war!"

Scott relaxed and Hentschell knew this was a sign for him to move.

"Lads!" began Scott. Hentschell moved in closer. The

other constables moved their hands to their truncheons. "... ya don't want t' fook with us, do ya? We know ya holding back som' details. So why dontcha just cuhme clean und tell us wot ya know now... before m' constables hav' t' git rough with ya!" Hentschell drew out his truncheon and glared at them.

"T'would be a pity to ruin your pretty lil' faces now, wouldn't it?" added Hentschell, raising his truncheon to Leigh's face and pointing at his nose. There was a two-inch scar on his left cheek. "Und... it looks like ya no stranger to a scar or two, are ya?"

Leigh looked at his younger brother. He knew his brother couldn't handle this kind of pressure for long. Joe's eyes erratically darted around the room, surveying the constables, then Scott and back to Leigh, seeking some sign of reassurance they were bluffing. The younger MacBride saw no reassuring nod or gaze from Leigh. Joe was a simpleton, clumsy and not very bright, but a hard-working farm labourer, nonetheless. The trouble with the MacBride brothers was their tendency to not recognize their limits at the local pub and become tit-faced at the drop of a hat. As DI Scott would say, "Som' peopl' should nev'r drink anyting but wartah. Alcohol for som' men is like an open flame to a moth; som' times dhey cuhn control dare course, but most of da time dhey cunnat..."

Scott stepped forward as Hentschell brandished his truncheon across the table in the faces of the MacBride brothers.

"Hentschell, take young Joe 'ere out of da room for a few minutes. I'd like to talk to 'is brudah alone."

Hentschell nodded and he took Joe by the arm and led him out of the room to a waiting area. The constables pointed to a chair and cuffed him to it while they stood guard outside the interrogation room. Scott's move had the desired effect on young Joe. He began to look concerned for his older brother. And although it was a decidedly cool spring day outside, beads of sweat popped out and zig-zagged down his weathered face. Inside the interrogation room, it was no less tense. DI Scott paced back and forth while Q held a truncheon within a hair's breadth of Leigh's head.

"Listen, Leigh… ya brudha's scared, we both know dhat. If I were a betting man, I'd say he'd tell us everyting he knows right aboot now… So why dontcha tell me und we won't hav' to put young Joe through any more trouble tonight."

"I told ya, I don't know nothin'," repeated Leigh. Q grabbed the other end of the truncheon and whipped it so fast under Leigh's neck and pulled hard back that Leigh groaned in pain and discomfort. It was a groan that young Joe could clearly hear from outside. Leigh tried to stand up, but Q's hefty weight prevented him from doing so.

"Steady on, boy!" exclaimed Constable O'Brien.

"Ya goin' nowhere tonight, not unless your brudah spills the beans, laddie. Why dontcha just make it easier fur 'im und tell us wot ya know?" continued Q. Outside, young Joe began to sweat more profusely, as the fear and uncertainty crept in. Inside the interrogation room, Q had placed a handkerchief in Leigh's mouth to prevent him from speaking further. Scott started to thud the walls and table with his large fists. Muffled sounds kept emanating from the room.

"Leave him be! He don't know nothin'. He weren't dare, I woz!" shouted Joe.

"Is dhat a fact!" exclaimed Hentschell. "Well, dhen, hold

on one moment, laddie, I tink DI Scott will want t' speak wid ya, right now!" The constable opened the door slowly and beckoned DI Scott to come out. Scott strode out of the room with his calabash gripped tightly in his right hand, still unlit. He moved briskly towards the constable, who whispered in his ear. Scott nodded and strode toward young Joe.

"Wot's dis I hear, Joe? Ya been a busy boy, 'ave ya? Tell me wot ya know before we 'ave to return to your brudah. Coz he's not a well man."

"I woz dare, okay? It woz me! Leave 'im alone! He knows nothin'."

"So, tell us wot ya know, Joseph MacBride! Und dis cuhn be all ov'r, und ya boys cuhn go home t' ya fadha!"

"He wanted a rifle. An Enfield; I told him I could git him one for da right price!" Scott moved closer to Joe and listened more intently.

"Who's *he*?" muttered Scott.

"I dunno his name, he never gave me a name. He told me t' meet him by da beach across from da Millings' hous'."

"Keep goin'…" continued Scott.

"Well, when I got dare… he woz waitin'. He wanted to try da rifle. So, he took a couple of rounds und shot 'em off at a couple of seagulls. The sun was going down and he wore a hat so I couldn't see 'is face good. He wasn't from around 'ere. He had a city accent."

"You expect me t' believe dhat ya don't know who dis man woz, dhat ya didn't see his face? Dhat seems incredible…" declared Scott incredulously.

"It's da god's honest truth! I swear it, on my muddah's soul!" retorted Joe. He appeared like a small child overshadowed by Scott's towering frame.

From inside the interrogation room, a sudden scuffle could be heard and a brief outburst as Leigh MacBride managed to free one hand and grab Q's pistol. Within seconds, he had squeezed off two rounds at the two constables in the waiting area, as the two constables drew their weapons fast and furiously returning a volley; one striking Leigh directly in the head and sending him flying backwards into the wall with such brute force it left an imprint in the horsehair plaster, as blood splattered across floor and wall. As the dust settled, two men lay lifeless. Joe was slumped over, with the chair still attached to his wrist by a dangling handcuff.

"Bloody 'ell!" yelled Scott as he got off the floor and dusted himself off. "Q?!" There was no response from the interrogation room. Hentschell and O'Brien moved cautiously toward the door with weapons drawn.

"Christ! Q! Q! He's duhne fur! Call the doctor!" declared O'Brien. Scott rushed into the room to find Q hunched over on the floor with a single shot to the face.

"Noooo! Q!" Scott yelled, rushing in to check for a pulse.

"No! Not dis! Dis can't be! Call Doc O'Grady and da coroner! Bloody hell…! Da MacBride's are donhe fur, dares no sign o' life! Und if ther' woz, I'd make bloody sure ther' wozn't fur long! Doze bastards!"

The station sat still for a long time before anyone broke the silence. Constable O'Brien offered a break in the prolonged and awkward stillness. He suggested delivering the news to Q's wife himself, since he knew Scott disliked this duty the most. Scott simply shook his head. He felt fully culpable for the events that transpired. Scott had known Q since he joined the Westport police force three years earlier. He was a prudent, eager and highly experienced constable. Scott knew his wife Bernadette well, and she would be utterly devastated. He dreaded delivering this news. Bernadette would collapse, just as Lilla Milling had earlier that day.

"Unudda widah in less dhan twenty-four hours!" mumbled Scott, as he stepped morosely from the station. He raised his calabash pipe to his pursed lips, as he contemplated the dismal few hours ahead.

The following morning, as DI Scott ambled towards the station, young Henry Desmond, the local paper boy, appeared. "Detective Inspect'r Scott! 'ere's da paypah!"

"Tank-ya, son!" handing the young lad a tuppence. "I trust your muddha und your faddha are doing well?"

"Yah, dhey send dare best wishes t' ya. I've gotta run now, Detective Inspect'r!"

The young lad scuttled off down a side street and disappeared into an alley. DI Scott watched as young Desmond Henry vanished out of sight. Scott looked down to the paper in his hand and flicked over to read the headlines:

MacBride Brothers Arrested in Connection to Murder of RM J.C. Milling!

"Bloody 'ell! Dhat's bloody wonderful now, isn't it?" Scott started to turn beet red, his face radiating heat on a chilly spring morning as steam appeared to pour off his skull.
"Good gawd! Dis is just wot da District Chief Inspect'r wants to see! He'll be knocking on m' door before da week is out... Wait till dhey git a load of dis mornin's events! Dis headline won't even compare to ta-morrah's!" Scott tucked the paper

into his coat pocket, filled his calabash with tobacco and struck a match before pondering his next move. He stood there peacefully gazing up at the wide blue, cloudless sky; gulls could be seen gliding in the distance over the shoreline. Several minutes passed before Scott took a bold, momentous leap forward.

Chapter Five
Veil of Secrecy

News of the events in Westport soon spread and eventually, as Scott had anticipated, word reached the office of the District Chief Inspector in Castlebar[1]. And it wasn't long afterwards that Scott received a telegraph summons to the District Chief Inspector's office in Castlebar. Perturbed by the summons, Scott's demeanour remained steadfast and confident of a favourable outcome in the imminent meeting with District Chief Inspector Marlowe.

District Chief Inspector Marlowe was a man in his sixties; his silver hair and moustache provided a distinguished appearance similar to that of a seasoned judge or politician. Marlowe was close to retirement. His successor could well have been DI Scott if politics and religion hadn't got in the way of Scott's advancement. DI Scott and the District Chief Inspector had a long, salubrious professional acquaintance for which both men held a mutual respect for one another. Marlowe, a known nationalist and supporter of an Irish-free state, while admiring Scott's tenacious, misguided loyalist sentiments, had no intention of recommending Scott for advancement. Marlowe had spoken to Scott on multiple occasions warning Scott of his *imprudent spiritual and political persuasions*. Scott chuckled at these words and would only offer that the Irish must learn to live with one another no matter what their religious or political persuasion. Scott added that a true Irishman and officer of the law serves the people without prejudice. Marlowe hemmed and hawed at Scott's naivety and admonished him for not understanding the nationalists' point of view. The way of the future, as Marlowe would say.

"One cannot act unbiased in dese matters. Yar Irish or yar not, DI Scott. Dare is no in between state."

DI Scott strongly believed that an Ireland separate from the Crown could only bring greater divide and sectarian violence between the Irish people. Scott, a devout, Plymouth brethren, drastically contrasted to Marlowe's catholic, nationalist beliefs. They often argued the points of differences between the two faiths. Two men joined by fate and their chosen professions to uphold the law yet divided greatly by religion and politics. And that was the crux of the sectarian struggles over the past centuries in Ireland. Even Marlowe's colleagues viewed him as a radical, bent to deliver his message skewed by salvation through conversion to the catholic faith and an Irish-free state. In Marlowe's own words, church and state were in fact indelibly linked and this would always be so.

DI Scott arrived early in Castlebar by way of D&SER's[2] Northern Line. As Scott stood on the platform waiting for his luggage, he drew his calabash out and lit it, taking a deep, resolute breath. The Castlebar train station was busy, with commuters and businessmen moving to and from the train. A young porter arrived with DI Scott's luggage — a gargantuan old, worn brown leather bag with Scott's initials on it and a single buckle securing it. The porter had to use both arms to lift it from the luggage trolley.

"'Ere you are, sir! 'Ave a wonderful dayh, sir!" puffed the porter. Scott emptied his pipe and tucked it in his pocket and took a tuppence from his trouser pocket and tossed it to the porter's open and eager hand. Scott simply nodded, grabbing the bag with one colossal paw while strolling off toward the street. The bewildered porter watched Scott walk away in one planetary stride, hailing a horse and buggy with his free hand.

It was 8:52 am on a Monday morning when DI Scott ambled into the District Inspector's office in the courthouse seated next to the Mall in the centre of town. The courthouse, built in 1834 with its wrought iron Greek Doric columns, bore all the gloomy austerity of the Victorian era. Deputy Chief Inspector Christian LaFleum was the first to greet DI Scott. The deputy chief inspector was a severe and slight fellow with beady, sullen brown eyes and ears that stuck up and outward like a mangy rodent. He had thinning light brown hair and small glasses perched upon a pompous, bulbous nose. All this contributed to an appearance that Scott often thought reminiscent of a weasel. This, coupled with the weasel's unpleasant disposition, provided Scott with enough fodder to remain firmly planted in Westport with like-minded, trustworthy individuals not motivated by political ambition, or self-aggrandizement.

The deputy chief inspector led DI Scott into a small waiting area with a couple of bleak-looking wooden chairs and a more inviting, large red leather reading chair outside Chief Inspector Marlowe's office. A young, buxom, red-haired lass omitting a faint scent of lavender about her manned a phone and a typewriter, huddled in the corner. She stood up, smiled coyly and offered DI Scott a cup of tea and a scone.

"No tank-you, miss, I 'ad som'sing earlier on da train up from Westport."

"DI Scott, I'll be right out. Please wait a second while I speak with Chief Inspector Marlowe first," announced the weasel, LaFleum. "I have som' unfinished bizniz widh da Chief." The weasel's intonation revealed an attempt to sound pragmatic yet urgent, but Scott saw through the charade. Scott acknowledged only with a quick nod as he returned his nonchalant gaze to the newspaper. The weasel opened the door to Marlowe's office after two brief knocks. Several minutes slid by interspersed with quick, short, mumbled exchanges. Scott half-heartedly tried to decipher the rambling joust of garbled words breaking the calm of the morning air. But he recognized quickly that knowing less in this case, made him far wiser.

Several more minutes of mumbled exchanges continued before an extended lull, followed by footsteps moving quickly toward the door. The handle turned slowly, and the weasel emerged with a stack of files under his arm. His head bowed down, he appeared to have a look of defeat as he shuffled past Scott and out of the waiting area. The red-haired lass stood and addressed DI Scott.

"Detective Inspect'r Scott, the District Chief Inspect'r will see ya now." She motioned for him to enter.

"Tank-ya, miss," declared Scott as he rose, cleared his throat and proceeded.

"Ahhh, DI Scott, I'm happy ya could make da long trek from Westport to see us in Castlebar today." The chief inspector was still looking down at his desk while he continued signing papers.

"Well, sir, I got 'ere as fast as I could, und as soon as I received ya summons."

"I see ya und yar lads 'ave bin very busy in Westport apprehending da criminal element," commented Marlowe.

There was a long pause before Scott answered. "Ahhh. Yes, sir, we're following som' solid leads dhat brought us t' som' suspects."

"I know of the MacBride brothers, DI Scott. Ya see, even in Castlebar, we keep well apprised of events in da boroughs. Ya might find dhat hard to fathom," declared Marlowe.

"No, sir, not at all. I believe I would do da same ting in your position. I tink dhat I understand da politics dhat drive deese affairs. I'm sure I'd follah some of da same interests if I were in ya shoes, sir."

"Indeed! Wud ya now?" laughed the chief inspector. "Indeed, ya wud, Mr. Scott!" The chief inspector finally looked up from his desk and gazed directly at Scott. Marlowe cleared his throat, straightened himself, and continued.

"Detective Inspector Scott, ya've bin a good detective und yar an admirable fella und I respect ya professionalism. Ya know ya 'ave m' utmost confidence und continued support."

"I'm happy to 'ave yar support und confidence as always, Chief Inspect'r," replied Scott.

"Let's understand each other clearly dough. Da Milling investigation, although a sad und unfortunate case, must be brought to a satisfactory end immediately. I know ya und Charles Milling were very close friends, und went through da Phoenix Park Training Depot[2] in Dublin together. But dare are udder forces at play 'ere. Doze I cunnat 'old back."

"Other forces, ya say?" DI Scott leaned forward in his chair and stared intently at the chief.

"Scott, we've known each uddah for over ten years now... und in those ten years 'ave I ever asked any professional or personal favours of ya?"

"Chief Inspector Marlowe, if yar asking me nat to pursue da perpetrators of dhis crime, I cunnat in all good conscience comply."

The chief inspector raised his eye glasses to his face and paused before answering. "DI Scott, I wouldn't 'ave expected ya to answer in any udder fashion; however, ya must understand I cunnat protect ya any furdha if ya pursue dis path ya 'ave wantonly chosen." He returned his gaze to the papers on his desk and continued signing more documents. Scott sat contemplating for several moments before standing.

"Well, Chief Inspect'r, I tank-ya fur ya time." Scott moved purposefully towards the door and stopped as he reached the threshold and removed his calabash. "Chief Inspector Marlowe, when I find da perpetrators of dis insidious, cowardly crime, no muddha where da trail takes me und m' men, we'll be sure to mention da support we got from da District Chief Inspector's office..." Scott tapped his pipe on the door frame and exited the office. Chief Inspector Marlowe gazed up from his desk and peered through his glasses just as DI Scott walked out. Marlowe threw the fountain pen he was holding across his desk and shook his head with disdain as he yelled out the office at the departing Scott.

"DI Scott! I'm tellin' ya, not asking ya! Bring dis case to an end swiftly, ya hear me!"

The train ride back to Westport unfolded cheerily, but crawled haltingly, weaving its way over the farmland. At times it seemed the great D&SER carriages floated upon a burdensome air of destiny. As the steam train thrust on, the sound of the track took on a pleasantly restful rhythm while Scott cogitated over his encounter with District Chief Inspector Marlowe. There was no question in Scott's mind that higher powers were somehow duplicitous in the murder of Charles Milling, but why and what motivation? The question at the forefront of Scott's mind was: how far reaching was this conspiracy? And who could Scott trust? Why had his friend John Milling been targeted? With Q's loss, he knew he'd soon receive a new constable from Phoenix Park Training Depot, one that District Chief Inspector Marlowe would appoint himself and would surely use to report directly back to Castlebar. Time was not on Scott's side, and he knew he needed to act fast.

DI Scott arrived back at the Westport police station a little before 2 o'clock in the afternoon. As he entered the station, he was greeted by young Constable Gormley — a brown-haired lad of about twenty years, a little over six feet tall and fresh out of the Phoenix Park training depot.

"Good morning, DI Scott, good t' see ya back. How woz your visit to da big city?"

"T' be honest widt ya, Constable Gormley, I wish I'd never left Westport. Meeting widh da district chief inspect'r woz far from auspicious…" Scott moved towards his desk with his calabash drawn. The cottage's old wooden beams gave the station a warmer appearance than its stark, bleak furnishings foretold. A single portrait of King George V hung above the fireplace. It appeared slightly discoloured from the soot of many a fire on damp winter days and hung slightly askew. There was a fire crackling away and Gormley had just placed a kettle on the stove to brew some tea. Scott plopped down in his chair and raised both feet on his desk. He lit his calabash and took a long deep breath, inhaling and studying the stack of files strewn before him. The train's whistle could be heard in the distance as it pulled slowly out of the station again en route to Belfast.

"List'n carefully, Gormley." Scott paused as Constable Gormley turned his attention to DI Scott. "I need to speak widh all da men today. Cun ya git messages to da lads to meet 'ere at 3 o'clock dis afternoon?" Gormley nodded and moved to the door, grabbing his overcoat and truncheon as he strode forward.

"I'll get da message t' all da lads und we'll be back as fast as I cun gaddah 'em, DI Scott."

"Mind ya-self, tell 'em dis meeting should be kept between us, police biz-niz, of course… ya know da drill."

"Understood, DI Scott! Consider it dunhe!"

Chapter Six
Scott versus the Nationalists

The Westport police station was crowded, with the remaining constables juxtaposed against the goliath, imposing figure of DI Scott. None of the constables were less than six feet, but next to Scott they all appeared distinctly Lilliputian by comparison. All seven men sat in a tight circle in the small station with Scott leaning forward. Scott had a pensive look. His men sat watching him in silence, knowing very well that a meeting such as this was a rarity and only called in times of great restiveness. DI Scott suddenly leaned back in his chair as he gazed into the faces of each of his young constables, moving his head in a counter clockwise direction. When he reached the last constable, he stood, cleared his throat and began…

"Ah-hem… Well, lads…" He paused before continuing. "Ya know dares a good reason fur ya all t' be 'ere today und I apologize fur da last-minute notice."

Scott continued by recounting the morning's events in Castlebar[1] with District Chief Inspector Marlowe. All the men focused intently on Scott like diminutive imps listening to the events of a bedtime story unfold. When Scott was done, he took out his calabash, pursed his lips in forethought before adding:

"Men, I tink ya should know dhat ya are all in danger by continuing along dis path widh me. But I must know dhat if ya decide t' stay — ya do so on ya own fruition. I'm not gonna press ya t' follow me und stay any longer on what will undoubtedly become anuddah tragedy da likes of da Titanic. Any man dhat wants to transfer to anudda borough is welcome t' do so t'day; und I will do everyting in my power to make dhat happen und not stand in yar way."

The constables all stood in unison before Scott could finish his sentence. Each spoke in turn and all vehemently agreed with the words of young Gormley — the first to speak.

"DI Scott, I swore to uphold da laws of da land und to da Crown no muddah wot. I am, und always will be, a constable in da RIC until da dayh I die. Ya just say da word, und I'll be dare standing by ya side." All the other constables nodded as Gormley finished. Scott made an unprecedented move and pulled out a bottle of whiskey and poured each of his men a dram and made a toast.

"'Ere's to ya men, widhout question da most honourable fellas a DI could hope to serve widh. I am honoured und humbled t' be in ya presence." Scott paused again before continuing. "Und dhat, I must say, woz da easy part. I need y' all t' be eva vigilant — look for any strangers t' Westport; keep ya eyes und ears open fur anyting unusual or out-of-place. Most important of all — I don't want any man t' work alone — from dis point onwards ya are to work in teams of two. Und dhat means ya eat, ya sleep und ya piss together! Understood? Und tap into any of ya usual informants fur more information surrounding da events of Milling's death; git on it und move fast lads. I 'ave a feeling we're all gonna be scrutinized very closely in da days und months t' follah. Und da sooner we put all dis t' bed, da better fur all of us!"

The night progressed with great sloth and mental turmoil for all men. DI Scott tossed and turned in his sleep as he awaited sunrise to creep through the curtains. His mind wouldn't quiet. There were so many unanswered questions and his meeting with Marlowe only succeeded by increasing his uneasiness. What could Marlowe be hiding? What role did Milling play for which he paid the ultimate price? Scott's mind was like a pendulum swinging first in one direction and then in another: was this more than just a radical group of nationalists bent on bringing civil unrest to the country? Or was this some kind of larger conspiracy? Not knowing who Scott could trust was the most frustrating. He knew it would eventually cause paranoia among his men as the weeks and months crept by and more pressure was felt from the powers that be in Castlebar. Scott had no illusions as to the lengths Marlowe, or those controlling Marlowe, could stoop.

DI Scott sat in his dining room drinking tea and pondering his next steps when a series of thunderous knocks struck his front door. He jumped up and approached, grabbing his Webley revolver. He moved to the front room and peered cautiously through the curtains and, upon seeing two of his constables on his doorstep, he lowered his pistol and proceeded.

He opened the door and was greeted by O'Brien and Gormley. "Sir, sorry to bother ya so early in da day, but we taught ya should know we 'ave a young replacement sent from da Phoenix Park Training Depot. A lad by da name of Jimmy Reilly. Seems like a quiet, harmless fella."

"Okay, lads. Let's look lively dhen. Remember, trust no one. I want ya lads to ensure dis tenderfoot isn't left alone und we watch 'im like a hawk. We may 'ave nothing t' worry about, lads. But in dis case, he's guilty until proven innocent."

"You needn't worry, DI Scott, we'll keep a good eye on dis lad. Und if he steps outta line even once, we'll be dare t' correct 'im," declared O'Brien.

"Good! Dhen da next order of bizniz is t' investigate our uddah leads, boys. Onward! Justice will prevail!"

Scott grabbed his coat and all three men set off for the Westport police station. It was a bleak and foggy morning in Westport, with the barely visible crest of Croagh Patrick a mere ten kilometres west of the town, poking out over the low clouds. Scott stopped abruptly before heading into the station and stared over at the summit of Croagh Patrick for several minutes. He thought of the mountain like an old adversary, both those he had met and those he would soon confront. He recalled the days of his youth when, just nine years old, he declared to his parents that he was going to climb to the summit of Croagh Patrick on his own. He recalled the words of his father...

"Well, son, if you must do it... dhen wot are ya waiting fur?"

And at that very instant, the young Scott grabbed his coat, hat and a flask filled with water, and set off to conquer Croagh Patrick. It was a little past noon when the young Scott set off and it wasn't till dusk, drenched to the bones, when the young lad returned to his home, where he was greeted by his mother and father seated in the dining room with a warm supper on the dining room table. His father was the first to speak:

"Und wot took ya so long, laddie? I woz aboot t' come up dhat littl' hill t' find ya." But before he could finish, Scott's mother piped up:

"Ah, dontcha list'n t' ya faddha, young William. He just got back from Croagh Patrick h'mself. Said he woz aboot twenty paces ahead of ya."

Scott was jarred back to present day by O'Brien and Gormley both addressing him at the same time. Neither of the constables knew how to interpret Scott's sudden trance-like state. It wasn't that they hadn't seen him detached and appearing to ponder something in his mind before, they just hadn't seen him transfixed so intently at Croagh Patrick. It was unsettling and surreal in nature, as if Scott were experiencing a premonition of sorts. This foreboding carried throughout the remainder of the day. As all three men entered the police station, young Reilly was nestled like a beetle under a rock behind Scott's desk. Reilly reclined in Scott's chair, his feet upon the desk. On Scott's desk sat a small, delicate letter among the files and scattered notes. Scott felt incensed that this little upstart, Reilly, sat in his chair with his feet up. And adding insult to injury, Reilly, appeared unperturbed at Scott's presence. Scott wondered what calibre of men the Phoenix Park Training Depot was sending out. He walked slowly over to his desk where Reilly sat, comfortable in his ignorance. By this time, Reilly seemed to discern the presence of an authority figure and he sat up and abruptly removed his feet from Scott's desk.

"Clearly, son, ya haven't spent mooch time in da boroughs?" announced Scott, as he towered over young Reilly with both hands firmly planted on his hips. His Webley leant forward in unison, somehow mimicking Scott's own quizzical squint. Young Reilly sat steadfast and unmoved, at least until DI Scott took his size thirteen shoe and whipped up the chair, sending Reilly flying sideways five feet across the room. O'Brien and Gormley chuckled by the front desk. As Scott turned to face them, he raised both eyebrows and almost cracked a smile as he pulled his chair back up and sat down squarely before tilting the chair back on two legs, with one enormous foot planted firmly on the edge of his desk. Scott focused on the letter taunting him on his desk and picked it up. Reilly seemed in a daze as O'Brien offered a hand to the young upstart. Reilly lay there for a second and dusted himself off before pushing O'Brien's hand away with utter disdain.

"Mind yourself, young lad!" was Scott's disapproving response to Reilly's complete disregard for any kind of peer respect. "Ya'll find yar days 'ere very long and arduous widh an attitude like dhat."

"Doncha worry about me, sir, I cuhn take care of m'self. Und I don't intend t' be gittin' comfortable amidst doze whom are loyalists needah." Reilly nodded towards the king's portrait hanging above the mantel.

"Ahhhh… let da truth be out, young Reilly! So, we 'ave a fine upstanding Nationalist among us, do we?" laughed Scott. "Dhat und a piss pot full of horse shit will git ya shot where I'm from, Reilly!" continued Scott, as he placed his Webley revolver on his desk with one almighty loud, determined thud. Reilly stood and walked over to DI Scott and handed him his transfer papers direct from Castlebar.

"Und just so we're clear, lad, I ain't worried abootcha one bloody bit. Hmmmm… wot's dis? I see our very own District

Chief Inspect'r Marlowe signed ya papers und look how he commends young Reilly so! Dhat's quite odd, ya sound like an entirely different fella from wot I've seen, laddie! Lemme set ya straight, boy! We've been waiting patiently for ya arrival. M' men will be watching ya like a hawk. Ya fall outta line for a moment und dhey 'ave m' permission t' kick ya behind from 'ere t' Dublin. Und I will be right behind 'em, laddie, to make sure ya don't bounce before ya land!"

Reilly stood silent for several moments as he reviewed the scene and seriously weighed his next move. He hadn't quite expected Scott's presence to be so commanding. He straightened himself, adjusting his tunic before addressing Scott with the respect that was due.

"DI Scott, I apologize for m' manners und any disrespect I 'ave shown. I will fulfil m' sworn duties as constable of dis borough."

"Indeed, you will, young Reilly. If dares one ting I cuhn be certain of… dhat ya will, lad… dhat ya will…! Und ya cuhn start by cleaning out da latrine." No sooner had Scott finished the sentence, a chorus of chuckles overcame both O'Brien and Gormley.

"Reilly, lemme show ya where da supplies are…" Reilly turned a darker shade of crimson and faced O'Brien as they moved off towards the latrine. No sooner had the two constables left, Scott turned his attention to the letter that sat oddly juxtaposed against the stark, plain manila case folders. He opened the letter carefully, noting the town postmark and date. The letter bore no return address, although that was not unusual in his line of business. It was not uncommon for the station to receive tips from concerned community members, especially in these times of growing public unrest in the face of nationalist sentiment. Scott and his men relied heavily upon these tips from loyalist sympathizers. However, they found it to be an increasingly tough battle to be fought against Sinn Fein and their call for recruits from the young and impressionable youth. A youth who saw no alternative than to join the Sinn Fein struggle for independence in the call for a prosperous and free Irish state, not bound by British rule.

Accompanying the letter was a faint, lavender scent. Scott took out a letter opener and tore the envelope, and carefully removed the contents. The type-written text caught his attention first. It was not customary for letters to be type-written, and suggested the originator was either a professional woman who had access to a typewriter, or possibly a lady of good standing in the community. Scott focused on the words and began reading. It was clear the person of origin was, in fact, not a lady of any particular social standing in the community, but rather a working-class woman. Scott concluded that this individual must be someone who had easy access to a typewriter, perhaps an office secretary. The faint scent of lavender was easily recognizable, and known to be frequently sold, at open air markets in Castlebar. He continued to read, and it was evident the originator of the letter was a credible and sincere source:

To whom it may concern:

I write to inform you and your men of a clandestine Sinn Fein meeting that will take place the evening 31st of March at the MacBride farm. Reliable information has come into my hands that in attendance at this meeting will be one Arthur Griffith[2]. Among his discussions with local sympathizers will *be seditious acts and recruitment of new members to Sinn Fein.*

I cannot hold in greater esteem the conduct of the Westport police, and appeal to you to remain vigilant and send any agent who may report directly to the Westport police any intelligence gathered.

Sincerely,
A concerned patriot

"Dhat's tonight!" deliberated Scott.

Scott pondered these words for several minutes, his eyes moving and scrutinizing each sentence with great deliberation. The words 'seditious acts' and 'Sinn Fein' stood out, and suggested this individual was no stranger to the politics of the day. He flipped the envelope over and checked the postmark again: *Castlebar!* Of course, the origin of the postmark might be nothing more than a red herring. But Scott was confident that this person was not trying to cover their identity.

Arthur Griffith was born at 61 Upper Dominick Street, Dublin on 31 March 1872. He was educated by the Irish Christian Brothers and early in his career he became involved in the Gaelic League, an organization that promoted the restoration of the Irish language. Griffith admired the late nineteenth century Irish nationalist, John Mitchel, who was known for his anti-liberalist rhetoric. Mitchel remained steadfast in his beliefs that an armed insurrection could only result in a massacre of those involved. Instead, Mitchel believed a passive resistance to English laws would be more fruitful in bringing down the system.

Arthur Griffith followed this very same philosophy. Griffith founded Sinn Fein in 1905 but distanced himself from the radical left of the day, who perceived the only way to establish a free-Irish state was through bloodshed and continued social upheaval. In the failed Easter Rising of 1916, Griffith took no part in the organization of the militia and openly criticized the whole affair, in which over four hundred people were killed. And in the aftermath of the events in Dublin, it became clear that the British army had become their own worst enemy in the wake of the murders of the likes of Francis Sheehy-Skeffington[3] and two innocent journalists. The path forward was clearly wrought with more bloodshed on both sides until some rational conclusion could be found. In Scott's mind, however, there could be only one resolution: squash the republican struggle for an independent free state. Nothing good could come of Ireland's independence from Britain. The irrational call from Sinn Fein to create an Ireland in which all were equal was nothing more than a radical plight. Northern Ireland's links with her colonial master were steadfast and indelibly ingrained into generations of the Irish people.

Scott waited for Reilly to return from his latrine cleaning and conjured up a new fictitious assignment.

"Constable Reilly!" yelled Scott from his desk. A few moments later Reilly appeared with a solemn look on his face. "Reilly, I take it ya 'ave cleaned out da latrine und ya are awaiting ya latest orders," smiled Scott. Reilly merely nodded in acknowledgement and straightened his jacket.

"Excellent, Reilly! Let's see what I 'ave fur ya! Hmmm, lemme see… it appears that Mrs. Kelliher is in need of some assistance. Her cat is stuck in a tree again. O'Brien, give Reilly the directions to Mrs. Kelliher's hous', would ya!" Reilly looked even more perturbed than before as he picked up his cap and truncheon and unceremoniously marched out the station.

No sooner had O'Brien led Reilly out of the station, Scott jumped to his feet and summonsed his remaining constables.

"List'n, men, we need t' act fast. I have just received an anonymous tip dhat nunhe uddah dhan our very own Mr. Arthur Griffith will be in Westport t'night attending a secret recruitment rally und future plans of sedition." Scott moved his eyes from man to man, before continuing:

"I 'ave formulated a plan dhat will require young Henry Desmond Shields t' play a role. Gormley, fetch young Henry Desmond 'ere immediately!" No sooner had the words left his mouth, Constable Gormley shot out the door and sped off like a tornado. The local Westport paperboy, Henry Desmond Shields, had always admired DI Scott and had professed on many occasions that when he was old enough, he wished to enlist in the RIC and enter as a cadet at the Phoenix Park training depot, just as DI Scott once did decades ago. Scott knew Henry Desmond was the ideal candidate for the plan he was hatching. He knew he could trust Henry Desmond, and this was just the kind of assignment the young lad would be thrilled about. True enough, when young Henry Desmond learned of his role in some important police business, he was beside himself in glory.

"Henry Desmond, ya understand how important ya role is? Remember, stay on ya guard at all times. Und dontcha wurry lad, me und m' men will be a stone's throw away, if dares any trouble. Ya know wot ya need t' do... I know ya cuhn do it und I trust in ya abilities as a young und capable agent of da Westport Police Force." Henry's eyes gleamed like two full moons in the night sky. "In fact," continued Scott, "I 'ave som'sing 'ere I wish t' give ya..." Scott opened his desk drawer and removed an old Westport police badge he had once received from his friend, John Milling, when he entered the Westport borough a few years prior. Scott placed it in Henry Desmond's hand:

"Dis is fur ya, Henry Desmond, but mind ya, keep it outta sight t'night. Undercover Agents of da Wesport Royal Irish Constabulary mustn't ever reveal dare true identity." Henry Desmond could barely hold back his excitement and seemed to devour every syllable that slid off Scott's tongue.

"DI Scott, ya und yar men can count on me! I will nat fail ya!"

It was dusk when Scott and his men convened outside the Westport police station. To ensure Henry Desmond's safety and to keep his role in the night's events clandestine, Scott had instructed Henry Desmond to remain home until dark and then make his way to the MacBride farm alone. He had asked Henry Desmond to tell his parents that there was a church meeting tonight for members of the choir. He assured young Henry being deceitful was permissible one time only in order to uphold justice and in keeping with the laws of public safety.

Young Henry Desmond arrived at the MacBride farm just as Scott had instructed. He was greeted at the large old barn by two strangers he'd never seen before in Westport.

"Boyo! Ya 'ere to enlist?" grunted the taller man wearing labourer's work clothes and boots. It was clear he was from the city — Henry Desmond thought perhaps the likes of a foreman for the public works department. Young Henry Desmond had acquired quite the talent for discerning people's occupations through simple observation, a talent he often shared with DI Scott when any stranger happened to be in town. Scott not only found young Henry Desmond's talents amusing, but he also provided the young lad with some basic tutelage in the art of observation. And this Scott found quite entertaining when he needed a diversion from his usual daily police affairs. Although Westport wasn't a bustling metropolis like Belfast or Dublin, the small town did see its share of travellers stopping off after a long haul from the south by train, along with the occasional tourist.

Accompanying the taller man, was a younger, stouter fellow with stubbly whiskers, also in labourer's clothing. They stood outside the barn with a roster in their hands, taking a count and asking for names. Henry Desmond approached and provided a false first and last name. The added danger to young Henry was that the town folk in attendance may well reveal Henry's close relationship with DI Scott and the game would be up. Scott resolved to remain close in case of trouble. As the pitch-black night sky thickened around them, Scott and his men remained hidden over a hundred yards away among the tree line that dotted the property boundary of the MacBride farm. Scott pulled out his telescope and watched intently as Henry entered the barn. He eyed the two men taking names outside and surveyed the townsfolk who arrived after Henry. This was a brilliant way to keep tabs on those who were in league with Sinn Fein. Scott pulled out a notebook and handed it to O'Brien who was crouched beside him.

"Take down deese names, O'Brien," whispered Scott. Scott proceeded to list several names of local townsfolk. He stopped abruptly as an automobile came to a flying halt alongside the barn and several men exited. Scott tracked the men with his telescope as they moved around to the front of the barn. The men were greeted with smiles and handshakes. And one man clearly appeared to be the centre of attention. He wore glasses and had black hair and a wide handlebar moustache. He was neatly dressed in a tailor-made, black pinstriped suit and shiny black shoes that reflected the moonlight. He carried a briefcase and was accompanied by two larger, stout men who looked like labourers and wore tweed caps. Scott noted a nasty scar on one of the men's faces as he turned momentarily to face the darkened tree line, all the while providing detailed descriptions to his scribe. Scott and his men had applied a liberal coat of black boot polish to their faces and hands in an effort to remain adequately camouflaged among the bushes.

"Ah, looks like Mr. Griffith has finally arrived..." whispered Scott to O'Brien. O'Brien passed the news along to the man next to him and so it went down the line.

After the final stragglers arrived and entered the barn, the two men holding the rosters got up from their chairs and entered. Scott motioned to his men to proceed forward, keeping a tight formation as they swooped in for closer surveillance. At that very instant, two men exited the barn with shotguns, and stood guard outside. Scott motioned for his men to back off and return to the tree line, where they remained until he summoned O'Brien forward. O'Brien was given the duty of moving in closer. The constables wore regular civilian clothing in the event that they were seen. And each man had doused copious quantities of whiskey on their clothes so as to provide a cover, if they were approached and questioned. All were artful in their ability to play a convincing drunkard, since each man had encountered drunks on many occasions as they went about their duties in Westport. Scott had further requested that some play the role of a chimneysweep and labourer by applying a liberal amount of soot and boot polish on their faces and hands — lending further credibility to their ruse in the event of discovery. Before O'Brien moved off, Scott pulled out a silver flask from his coat pocket. He handed it to O'Brien and motioned for him to take a drink. The smell of whiskey was clear as the moonlit night on his breath as he moved away at a stealthy crawl.

It was several minutes before O'Brien was within twenty yards of the barn, Scott steering a cautious eye on the guards outside as he moved closer, crouching and crawling through the undergrowth. He beckoned to the three men at the end of their formation to move in from behind the barn and they set off, crawling again at a stealthy pace. The two guards now lit cigarettes and were talking, not paying any attention to the direction from where O'Brien was approaching. Constable O'Brien lay within a few yards of the chicken coup, the hens clucking and strutting around, pecking intermittently at the ground for specks of grain. O'Brien moved closer, nestling only inches from the chicken coup. The moonlight reflected off the cattle troughs. Scott surveyed O'Brien's progress and the two guards; his telescope moving expeditiously from one subject to the other. They waited patiently, hardly breathing for any sign of jeopardy. He instructed his remaining men to advance toward the barn at a slow crawl. Scott moved first, leading his constables. They stopped every few yards to take stock of their progress and ensure they remained undetected.

Towards the back of the barn, young Henry was seated between two short, burly fellows. One of the men had a distinct odour of whiskey, while the other balding man had two tattoos on both exposed forearms — one an anchor and the other a rather scantily-clad, young lady. Young Henry Desmond knew instantly from this man's appearance, the size of his forearms and the choice of tattoos, that he was a fisherman. Arthur Griffith was introduced by the local Sinn Fein representative and seated beside him at the front was none other than old man MacBride. The turnout was pretty respectable for Westport and as Henry Desmond noted, there appeared to be many men and young boys from local townships who had made the trek to Westport for this event. In all, young Henry Desmond estimated there was between forty-two and forty-eight people in the MacBride barn. Mr. Arthur Griffith was unquestionably a crowd-puller. After introductions, Griffith heralded the local Sinn Fein representatives from neighbouring townships. A short pause followed as Mr. Griffith cleared his throat and took a drink from a glass of water sitting on some wooden crates serving as a makeshift podium.

"I tank-ya all fur coming t'night esp'cially ta doze who 'ave come great distances t' be 'ere. I am humbled t' be in ya presence. We Irish 'ave long endured da tyranny of the British." The opening words incited a rally of raucous rants and bellowing jeers from the crowd. Young Henry Desmond sat patiently and silently but managed to raise a reluctant fist in defiance so as not to draw unnecessary attention. The man to Henry's left smiled approvingly as he glanced over at the young lad. Henry was intent on his mission. He purveyed those close to the front and took mental notes of their appearances; he carefully noted their approximate height, build, hair colour and best guess at their occupations. Many vocations were easy enough to discern since many fisherman and labourers lived and worked in neighbouring towns and villages. A couple of insidious looking fellows were seated to the right of the makeshift crate podium facing the crowd. Henry didn't recognize them as locals, their hands overshadowing their even larger forearms. Each forearm bore tattoos, but Henry couldn't make out the tattooed figures that adorned the men. He was sure both were labourers, probably brickies judging by the amount of dust on their clothes and the size of their upper torsos and forearms.

Henry himself was a slightly built young boy, with light brown mousy hair and bright, curious green eyes. Freckles dotted his cheeks and nose, and he always wore clothes that were just a touch too big, since he usually got his older brothers' hand-me-downs. The money he earned graciously handed over to his parents to help support the family, just as his older brother, Shaun, had done before him. Both his parents had jobs — his mother a seamstress and his father a fisherman in a local township to the east. Henry Desmond had been the local paperboy in Westport for three years — a much sought after job for young boys his age. Henry had a recognizable face. As such, he wore his cap low on his brow and at Scott's behest, he had smudged enough soot on his face, hands and clothes so as to appear a chimney-sweep's apprentice. Every time old man MacBride turned to survey the crowd gathered in his barn, young Henry quickly glanced down at his feet to dodge the old man's line of sight or he'd obscured himself behind a stout man sitting in front.

After several more welcoming words from Arthur Griffith, accompanied by the local Sinn Fein representatives, they hastily moved onto the prospect of new recruits. One local representative spoke of seditious acts on the Crown, and these words resonated in Henry Desmond's ears like bullets from a shotgun echoing in an open field. And although Arthur Griffith seemed to look on in disapproval, he did not speak up in protest. Henry Desmond noted this and understood that when any public gathering even alluded to this subject, it was illegal and those responsible could be brought swiftly to justice circumventing the civil courts with the introduction of the Restoration of Order in Ireland Act that had become effective in August of 1920. Henry Desmond knew Scott wasn't the kind of man who would sanction the imprisonment of anyone simply for their political persuasion, no matter how misguided that person might be; rather, Scott was more concerned with justice for the men responsible for his friend's murder. And if Scott was able to identify those nationalist elements hidden among his jurisdiction, then he'd be in a more advantageous position. Arthur Griffith, although a well-known nationalist and supporter of an Irish free state, was equally well-known for his stance against any kind of armed resistance. And although Griffith spoke many times in public about the senseless deaths of those involved in the Fenian Rising[4], and outwardly appeared to oppose this violent upheaval, he never made any attempt at an official condemnation of such acts.

Outside, Constable O'Brien positioned himself next to the barn and could clearly hear every word coming through the broken or missing wooden slats. From Scott's vantage point, he could see the two guards out front moving around after they had extinguished their cigarettes. They had picked up their shotguns and were cradling the weapons in their arms like newborn babes. One of the guards moved dangerously close to where O'Brien was concealed but turned at the very last second. O'Brien kept track of the guards while listening intently to the words echoing from the barn. He peered through one broken slat to see the crowd neatly gathered inside. For one brief moment he believed he saw young Henry Desmond, but poor lighting made it impossible to say. There was a sudden shout of disapproval from the chairs towards the back of the barn as one young boy stood up and pointed to young Henry Desmond. Suddenly, a scuffle broke out as two seated men at the back swooped in on young Henry and grabbed him by the wrist, quickly pulling him outside the barn, out of sight from the crowd's attention. Griffith continued on, unfazed by the commotion taking place at the back of the barn.

Scott responded decisively as the two brutes pulled young Henry outside and began to berate and question him. The guards moved in closer to young Henry, obscuring him from Scott's line of sight. From a short distance away, Scott and his men with weapons drawn, charged the four guards leading his squad forward, they laid in full force like a freight train. The guards turned, swinging their shotguns around to face the onslaught of a mass of charging constables. The two men who had pulled Henry outside, turned and ran towards the barn to sound the alarm. The undetected O'Brien pounced with firearm poised; he moved with lightning agility to cover his colleagues' forward advance. Scott knew he and his men were easily outnumbered by the size of the crowd inside the barn, although they had two advantages: the element of surprise and a greater force of weapons. The two guards quickly threw down their shotguns upon seeing Scott leading the charge in the midst of a line of constables, just as O'Brien turned the corner to meet the two guards rushing to warn the others. He stopped them abruptly, pointing his Webley squarely as they hastily discarded their weapons. The crowd inside still oblivious to the events unfolding outside. Griffith could be heard addressing the crowd among loud jeers and applause.

Young Henry Desmond moved forward to provide Scott with enough information that he needed to legally process those gathered inside: *seditious acts* was the term Scott sort. Young Henry Desmond thanked Scott for his fast actions.

Scott nodded at the lad: "Tank-ya son! Now, ya best be on ya way home befor' ya Ma and Fadha call da alarm! I'll see ya t'morrah laddie!' He patted Henry on the shoulder, as the boy strolled off into the moonlight, looking back occasionally to witness the unfolding melee. Scott was now acutely aware his presence would be construed as an aggressive stance taken by one lone detective inspector in the boroughs. He envisioned the biased press and melodramatic headlines to follow, although it was a risk he had calculated and understood clearly. All that was left was to process the crowds inside and issue their citations. Scott and his constables strolled inside, while O'Brien handcuffed the guards and sat them down in the dirt back-to-back.

As Scott and his constables walked inside the barn, Arthur

Griffith stopped abruptly in mid-sentence, shaking his head in disapproval. The crowd turned their heads simultaneously, with some standing up and others yelling epithets at Scott and his men as they entered. Undaunted, Scott strode purposefully forward to address the crowd and holstered his pistol.

"Quiet down! Quiet down lads! As I understand it, all of ya are gathered 'ere t'day t' discuss seditious acts upon da Crown." Arthur Griffith jumped in to interrupt amid even louder jeers and taunts from the agitated crowd.

"Detective Inspect'r, we're gathered 'ere tonight t' discuss da relevance of continued home rule in a state dhat needs nuhn; dhat, und… future crop rotation." This was met with a wave of resounding laugher. Griffith continued, "Woteva you 'ave bin led t' believe is untrue, und I will remain steadfast in my admonitions of ya und yar constables in obstructing a peaceful public gathering of like-minded individuals." Scott wasted no time in firing back a powerful volley.

"Mr. Griffith, I'm under no illusion as to yar resolute hypocrisy. In fact, as I understand it, ya 'ave bin so steadfast in ya wholesale lack of publicly condemning seditious acts upon da Crown dhat ya 'ave brought down many an Irishman in violent and bloody acts against one anudder as a result. I must step up as my duty calls und uphold both da law und protect doze innocent Irishmen und women who wish to live in peace widthout further wanton and needless bloodshed. A free Irish state may well cuhm some dayh; und it may well cuhm to a sectarian divided Ireland, but I cuhn only hope I am six feet under if dhat ever cuhmes to pass. A true Irishman fights not for wot he cunnat change, by murdering 'is bruddahs. Once ya start duhne dhat path, ya've already lost da battle!"

The crowd in the barn suddenly grew morosely silent. Some of the men bowed their heads, picked up their hats and jackets, stood solemnly and walked outside to the waiting constables who took their names, occupations, employers, addresses and brief descriptions before releasing each man into the murky night. A dense and ominous fog had drifted into the field surrounding the MacBride barn and as men departed, it created an eerie sensation as they appeared to melt away into the fog like ghostly apparitions never to be seen again.

Chapter Seven
Maud Gonne

William Butler Yeats and Maud Gonne met one light and breezy day in London at the Hermetic Order of the Golden Dawn. This was an organization devoted to the study and practice of the occult, metaphysics, and paranormal activities that had been active during the late 19th and early 20th centuries. Also known as a magical order, the Hermetic Order of the Golden Dawn (or The Golden Dawn) was active in Great Britain and focused its practices on theurgy and spiritual development. Yeats had instantly fallen for Maud. She became a tumultuous and stormy attraction for Yeats that was doomed to failure from the onset. Maud was born at Tongham, near Farnham in Surrey county, as Edith Maud Gonne, the eldest daughter of Captain Thomas Gonne (1835–1886) of the 17th Lancers, whose ancestors hailed from Caithness in Scotland, and his wife, Edith Frith Gonne, born Cook (1844–1871). Maud's mother died while she was only four years old. Her father then sent her to a boarding school in France to be educated. Maud once wrote: *"The Gonne's came from County Mayo, but my great-great grandfather was disinherited and sought fortune abroad trading in Spanish wine. My grandfather was head of a prosperous firm with houses in London and Oporto -- he*

*destined my father to take charge of the foreign business and
had him educated abroad. My father spoke six languages but
had little taste for business, so he got a commission in the
English army; his gift for languages secured for him
diplomatic appointments in Austria, the Balkans and Russia,
and he was as much at home in Paris as in Dublin."*

As youngsters, Maud and her younger sister, Kathleen,
often travelled with their nurse to London to visit her mother's
relatives, where they were exposed to a very different lifestyle.
They despised these visits, preferring to play free in Ireland.
As Maud later recounted: *"We hated these visits after our free
Irish life, where we were allowed to play with the children of
the many mud cabins which existed then everywhere."* Perhaps
it was this combination of childhood influences and a foreign
education that fermented the seeds of alienation, indifference
to her homeland and eventual participation in the Irish
nationalist movement. Maud definitely cultivated an active
interest in an Irish free state governed by Home Rule. She was
a somewhat masculine and plain woman, yet Yeats was
infatuated with her, though he didn't confess the same
sentiments for an Irish free state.

"William dearest, I cannot marry you!" Maud
emphatically declared. "You see, I am your muse, and must be
no more."

"I implore you, Maud, I will not cease my protestations to
the contrary!" responded Yeats.

"You may not, and I shall not be persuaded! Dear William,
it is not our fate to join in holy matrimony. And besides, you
are insufficiently nationalistic for my tastes!"

"But my darling Maud, with you my muse is limitless.

Without you I am not happy," protested Yeats.

"Oh yes, you are, William dearest. Because you make beautiful poetry of what you call your unhappiness and are content in that. Marriage would be such a dull affair, Poets should never, ever marry. The world should thank me for not marrying you! Mark me well, and you and your muse may thank me some day too!" The very words falling from Maud's lips engulfed his entire being, leaving him in an eternal darkness from which he never fully recovered. They parted that solemn evening, with Maud simply kissing Yeats on the cheek before stepping out; leaving poor Yeats to return to his writing desk and recount the many times Maud had refused his proposals. He was a man obsessed with every single inch of Maud and all that she embodied in life and soul. There was nothing he would not perceive of undertaking for her. A week later news of Maud's marriage to John MacBride was announced in Le Figaro[1]. Yeats took the finality of this news deep to his core, inspiring several poems with Maud clearly the intended subject.

Maud's marriage to John MacBride was short lived, but not before he had confided in her his intent to return to Ireland to join the Irish nationalists in an armed insurrection against the British. However, one obstacle remained for John's success: the British knew John MacBride well from his days commanding the Irish Transvaal Brigade. He would be closely watched by the authorities upon his return to Ireland. Nonetheless, MacBride returned to Dublin after his divorce from Maud in 1905. Maud approved of John's move and the part he would eventually play in the Easter Rising. And although their divorce was far from acrimonious, W.B. Yeats never forgave John for his illicit treatment of Maud. Maud however, sent her ex-husband gleefully off with a suitcase full of francs to assist in the nationalist cause and eventual liberation from British home rule.

The aftermath of the Easter Rising of 1916, and MacBride's execution by the British saw Maud return to Ireland with the sole intent of raising more funds for the nationalist cause. She approached Arthur Griffith with a sole proposal of becoming their fundraiser by travelling to America and further soliciting the Irish American social elite where funds had been pouring in quite generously over the years to the Irish nationalists. But of late the coffers had been slowly diminishing — requiring a further injection to move the nationalists' fight forward and bring reparation for the injustices of the past.

Chapter Eight
The Initiation of Joe Fáinne

Joe Fáinne was born out of wedlock in an impoverished Northside neighbourhood of Dublin. Accounts from his mother suggested Joe's father was a labourer, but word on the street pointed to the fact that he was no more than a common thief. His young mother had left Joe in his father's care and reportedly moved west to live with distant relatives. The young Joe learned quickly and fought boys from his neighbourhood countless times if they even dared to think his father was a thief. Joe learned to be street savvy from a very early age. He graduated from common thievery to assault and battery before he was seventeen, quite the accomplishment even for a young lad from the Northside. In fact, Joe had spent the majority of his adult life in Bridewell remand facility and later he was transferred to Kilmainham Gaol[1]. Kilmainham had a reputation of dire prison conditions and within its walls it was not uncommon for men, women and even children to be incarcerated up to five per cell, unsegregated. Many of the revolutionaries of the Easter Rising of 1916[2] were held in Kilmainham Gaol where they were swiftly executed by the British. Public hangings were held in front of Kilmainham Gaol, but by the 1820s these State-sanctioned displays of brutality became less common, perhaps less socially acceptable. As a result, a single cell on the first floor between the West and East wings was built in 1891 to accommodate private hangings.

Shortly after the Easter Rising, young Joe Fáinne was reborn, graduating from common criminal to separatist. At Kilmainham Gaol, Joe met fellow inmate, Eamon De Valera[3], who had been sentenced to death after his role as a rebel leader during the Easter Rising of 1916. Fortunately for Eamon, the sentence was commuted to life after his case had been reviewed and De Valera was deemed unimportant and of no obvious future threat. And the two men struck up a friendship based upon a shared necessity. Joe supplied Eamon with contraband, such as cigarettes and newspapers, while Eamon kindled Joe's hatred of the British, bringing with it a new sense of motivation by the nationalist movement upon his release from Kilmainham. Joe had long blamed the British for his own pathetic circumstances, believing under British home rule the Irish were all second-class citizens and no Irishman could possibly be elevated in society. When De Valera was transferred to Dartmouth prison, Joe was coincidently due to be released. Before De Valera was scheduled to be transferred, he instructed young Joe to seek out John Devoy[4] or Michael Collins[5]. De Valera said they would find a sanctuary for Joe and provide him with a profitable new vocation.

Following the failed Easter Rising, public opinion quickly turned against the British in the wake of the executions of many rebel leaders. Scott earnestly followed the events in Dublin and even he was alarmed at the brutality of the British in the reports being published in the boroughs. He viewed the Irish Republican Brotherhood and the Irish Republican Army

(IRA) as nothing more than a nuisance from afar, but now this minor vexation had hit close to home. Unbeknown to DI Scott, Arthur Griffith had set into motion a plan before his arrest and for which Joe Fáinne would eventually play a pivotal role. Griffith met with several members of the Irish Republican Brotherhood prior to the Easter Rising and he left detailed plans for subversion in the capable hands of John Devoy. He was leader of the Clan na Gael[6], the Irish republican organization active in the United States in the late 19th and 20th centuries and the successor to the Fenian Brotherhood and sister organization to the Irish Republican Brotherhood. Devoy recruited volunteers for various assignments across Ireland. Devoy, in collaboration with Michael Collins, established a paramilitary-style squad that later became known as the Michael Collins Squad. The squad was responsible for many attacks on local RIC barracks and is suspected of multiple assassinations of prominent Unionists in Northern Ireland.

On the morning of May 3rd, 1917, Joe Fáinne was released from Kilmainham Jail just a stone's throw away from the Phoenix Park Training Depot, as two strange men in suits approached.

"You're Joe Fáinne, aren't you?" announced the first man in a noticeably distinctive upper-class British accent as he tipped his hat. Joe eyed the two strangers suspiciously.

"I'm sorry, that's very rude of me. I'm Bill Mitchell and this is my colleague, John Blithe." Blithe nodded and tipped his hat. "We're from Army Intelligence and we'd like a quick chat with you." Joe had been briefed by De Valera and he knew exactly how to respond.

"I'm sorry, lads, but I've got a funeral to git tah."

"A funeral, you say? Ahhh." interjected Blithe, the taller of the two men. He removed his hat and continued. "Well, it won't take up much of your time, I can assure you. We just want to ask you a few questions."

"Like I said, boys, I 'ave a funeral to git tah and me train will b' leaving soon." Joe adjusted his cap and pushed past the two men.

"We'll be watching you, Mr. Fáinne. You can be sure of that." Joe looked back over his shoulder and grinned maniacally at the two men. The British agents stood motionless, watching as Joe Fáinne disappeared towards the centre of the city.

Joe met John Devoy at a predetermined location that was coincidently merely yards from Café Cairo[7] on Grafton Street. Devoy extended a hand as Joe approached.

"Pleased to meet ya. Joe Fáinne, is it?" Devoy was a man in his mid-fifties with a bulbous nose and thick wavy brown hair, and he wore an unkempt beard that gave him the appearance of a schooner captain. Born in County Kildare, Devoy travelled to France in 1861, where he joined the French Foreign Legion and briefly served a year in Algeria before returning to Ireland and becoming active in the Irish Republican Brotherhood. There were rumours that Devoy had been dishonourably discharged from his duties.

"Pleased t'meet ya, John," offered Joe in return. In comparison to Devoy's firm handshake, Joe's was entirely limp and feathery. Devoy had already judged the man before their greeting concluded.

"Follow me, lad," instructed Devoy. "Und we'll find ya a roof ov'r ya head, und tah-morrah we'll find ya som'sing to occupy ya-self widh."

Joe spent the night at the home of a young working-class Dublin couple who were republican sympathizers. The next morning Joe found the old, abandoned warehouse where he met with John Devoy and several other men whose names were never divulged. Fear of British counterintelligence and reprisals from the authorities were top among their discussions. And the men were careful not to use first or last names. Devoy proceeded to outline a plan devised by Michael Collins following the executions of several of the rebel leaders arrested in the aftermath of the failed Easter Rising. Collins' plan called for volunteers to undergo training in Ballymote, a small market town about 81 kilometres northeast of Westport. Joe was one of several men who agreed to travel northwest by train the very next morning for eight weeks' intensive training.

Chapter Nine
The Milling Tax

A cool spring morning descended upon Westport, DI Scott sat squarely behind his desk with a cup of tea balanced precariously on a stack of neatly piled, badly worn manila folders. His attention focused upon one open manila folder sprawled among many others. At the forefront of his mind was the capture of the perpetrators of the crime at hand. As Scott perused the documents laying across his desk, he realized one name stood out among many. He'd seen this name before in another document — but where? He started flipping through pages of court documents feverishly. Suddenly, it occurred to him that this person of interest, one Joseph Fáinne, had appeared in court before the Honourable John Milling. Scott flipped over the folders and pushed the documents around on his desk in a frenetic search for the elusive report he sought. His eyes shifted quickly and suddenly the name he sought jumped out in a court document dating back to March 1918. In it, several men, including Joseph Fáinne, were arrested after protesting the arrest of another volunteer, Ned Moane, after being held for unlawful assembly and illegal drilling. The Sinn Fein movement had grown steadily in Westport since the Easter Rising and both Ned Moane and Joe Fáinne were prominent members. Scott continued scanning the report. The account detailed the defiance shown by all the defendants as they turned their backs in court on the Honourable John Charles Milling. It wasn't until Milling had requested several constables be brought into the court room, when all the defendants were forcibly turned to face the court. Joe Fáinne wore a volunteer's cap but vehemently refused to remove it during the proceedings. All men were sentenced to twelve months' hard labour.

DI Scott combed his desk some more, until he found the list of those who had attended the Sinn Féin meeting at the MacBride farm. He scanned the list and stopped abruptly when he reached the name in question. Scott requested the arrest records of Joe Fáinne, which placed him in prison at the same time as Eamon De Valera. Upon finding Joe Fáinne on the list, he was convinced beyond any doubt that he had found one possible suspect in Milling's murder. Scott summoned his constables immediately. He stood with his men huddled around his desk momentarily and started to pace back and forth as the constables waited patiently for their leader to break the silence. They watched every move Scott made, as he raised his pipe to his lips taking one long, deep inhalation of tobacco. Scott stopped abruptly and removed the pipe from his mouth, pursing his lips in contemplation before speaking.

"Is that young upstart, Reilly still out on his rounds?"

"Yes sir!" declared Hentschell.

"Good job lads!" responded Scott, smiling. "We're gittin' closer lads! Dis fella, Joseph Fáinne, appears to fit da profile of a potential suspect." Scott passed the file to O'Brien, now sitting to his right. He opened the file, scanned it, and in turn passed it onto the next constable. The file completed its circuit before Scott announced, "I want dis suspect brought in fur questioning immediately. We'll need to track dis fella down since he only provided a Dublin address, which I suspect is entirely fictional. I will follow up on dis lead in Dublin m'self."

O'Brien was the first to speak up, "Perhaps, sir, I can join ya, if'n ya plan t' head t' da city?"

"Tank-ya fur da offah, O'Brien, I would be happy for som' company!" replied Scott. "Now list'n 'ere lads, dare's never bin a time fur ya all t' remain ever vigilant... Keep ya eyes peeled und use all ya resources t' find dis fella. He 'as da answers, I cunh feel it in m' bones. O'Brien and I will leave tah-morrah for Dublin."

Scott's mind drifted momentarily from the intricacies of the case to that of the Milling widow and child. He knew what he should do and wasted no further time. He scooped up his coat and hat with one giant swipe and galloped out of the station. The constables sat watching as the towering figure moved in one momentous cyclonic stride out the door and whirled down the street in a tempestuous roar of boots hitting cobbled stone. The constables exchanged brief, curious looks, with several men's eyebrows furrowed with quizzical expressions. They had never seen Scott move more deliberately in one full sweeping, unobstructed manner. A momentary tranquillity filled the room before several men stood up, gathered their hats and coats, and left in their designated pairs in search of any information that may lead them to Joe Fáinne or any of his known associates.

Scott was missing for over twenty-four hours before resurfacing. It wasn't until several weeks later when Scott's mysterious disappearance could be explained. Accounts from the office of District Chief Inspector Marlowe detailed how DI Scott petitioned the court in Castlebar on Lilla's behalf for a widow's compensation in the amount of six thousand pounds, which the court eventually granted under protest from town representatives and some anti-unionist elements, set against any kind of financial retribution awarded to an apparent loyalist and their next of kin. The funds were eventually levied on the towns of Westport and the County Mayo Council. And although there were multiple objections from representatives from Westport and the County Mayo Council, the court's decision was final. In the aftermath of the decision, locals soon dubbed this additional tax burden as the *Milling tax[1]*.

Finally, the inevitable and solemn day in Westport arrived when Lilla and Maggie Milling moved to Armagh. Lilla's grief had so consumed her that she had not been able to attend her husband's funeral, but DI Scott reported back to Lilla that the Marchioness of Sligo and Lord Altamont[2] were present at John's funeral, which seemed to provide some solace to young Lilla. DI Scott had grown fond of Lilla and little Maggie, and amidst the sorrow of losing the presence of a close friend and confidant, he cheerfully said his goodbyes and promised to visit them when they were comfortably settled into their new home. Little Maggie Milling remained quiet and more introverted than ever since her father's murder. Lilla had disclosed to DI Scott that Maggie had witnessed her father's murder as he stood with his back to the window winding the grandfather clock in their drawing room. As the sounds of gunshots rang out in the Milling home[3] at dusk, Lilla ran from the kitchen to the drawing room only to find her husband propped up awkwardly against a wall, with a bloodied shoulder and stomach wounds, with young Maggie sobbing and screaming: "Daddah! Daddah!"

Chapter Ten
The Conspiracy

DI Scott was still troubled by his meeting with District Chief Inspector Marlowe. He knew Marlowe's political tendencies leaned awkwardly towards the separatist left, but he wondered what other political motives may be involved and how far reaching the Milling conspiracy could stretch. Scott decided there and then that he must focus on bringing the perpetrators of this crime to justice and nothing else. He was certain that all the other pieces to this puzzle would fall neatly into place in due course. He resolved to follow the path he had set out on, knowing fully well that this may lead him and his men to an unenviable fate, or at the very least an abrupt and career-ending thud.

Scott and O'Brien set out for Dublin the following morning on the D&SER[1] train via Castlebar. As the two men sat in the front carriage across from one another, Scott pulled out his calabash and laid it neatly on the seat next to him. He then undressed a tightly wound pouch of tobacco held together by a worn piece of yarn. He held the tobacco under his nose momentarily and inhaled the scent of a nicely aged Kent. He perched the pipe between forefinger and thumb, and with his left hand he pinched a precise quantity of tobacco and stuffed it judiciously into the chamber. Tiny flecks of tobacco could be seen peeking over the pipe bowl as Scott simultaneously struck a match while inhaling through the lip. Instantaneously, the carriage filled with a warming and welcoming scent of burning tobacco. It annoyed some passengers, particularly some of the ladies, as they gathered up their belongings and left the carriage in a decidedly uncourteous huff. And although O'Brien was not partial to the smell of tobacco himself, even he felt sheathed in satisfaction from Scott's pipe — reminding O'Brien so much of his late grandfather.

It was late afternoon when they arrived in Dublin. As the train pulled into the station, a small crowd of reporters gathered and appeared to huddle together in close conference. Two men broke away from the crowd with Kodak No. 1A cameras in tow and waited for the train to stop while its passengers disembarked. Scott and O'Brien grabbed their luggage and readied themselves for the onslaught awaiting them. As they alighted the carriage onto the platform, Scott's massive hulk towered over everyone; the reporters and two photographers swarmed upon the two men.

"Detective Inspector Scott! I'm James Munroe from the Irish Times. Would you 'ave a mo'ent to speak t' us about the untimely deaths of the MacBride brothers under your care?"

Other reporters streamed forward, jostling for better vantage points within earshot to Scott and O'Brien.

"DI Scott! Liam Edwards from the Evening Herald! Are you 'ere to meet with the Chief District Inspector? What was MacBride's involvement in the murder of the Honourable John Charles Milling?"

Both Scott and O'Brien mowed purposefully through the crowd without as much as a single utterance, with the reporters and photographers in close pursuit. Scott pursed his lips, holding up his giant paw, peering through the pack of journalists, simply announcing: "Gentl'men please! M' constable und I are nat 'ere to mollify da needs o' salacious hearsay, n'muttah wot da source. I might 'lso add, we cunnat comment on police investigations still underway." O'Brien smiled and followed in his mentor's giant wake as Scott plowed through the gathering press.

They moved quickly and eventually lost the reporters' interest as they approached 22 Upper O'Connell Street in the centre of Dublin to find lodgings at the Gresham Hotel[2] for the night. After they dropped their belongings in their rooms, Scott and O'Brien cautiously set out in search of the mysterious address on record for Joe Fáinne. Constable O'Brien wore his civvies, so as to remain inconspicuous. They carried their Webley's in their inside pockets. Scott and O'Brien were acutely aware of the civil unrest that had plagued the city for several months. And the presence of two RIC policemen searching for clues may only incite further troubles as they crossed from white-collar to blue-collar Dublin neighbourhoods. Passing over the River Liffey from north to south Dublin, the social-economic divide transformed dramatically from prestigious and progressive neighbourhoods to tightly packed, red brick tenements where unsavoury, ragged looking characters propped up the doorways and lurked in lurid alleyways. Even the air seemed to grow distinctly thicker as they passed through squalid neighbourhoods, with lingering odours of unknown origin that offended even the more seasoned veteran of the streets.

The two men moved guardedly through open

marketplaces where vendors yelled out to draw potential customers. Their senses were so accosted by such a variety of smells, sounds and sights that their pace almost slowed to a crawl through the dense, languid air. A rank smell of fish surrounded them momentarily before a short, brief breeze diminished the powerful odour. Dusk fast approached and some street vendors began packing away their wares for the night. Scott and O'Brien arrived at the abode on record for Joe Fáinne. Scott suggested they observe the address before attempting to approach the door and question its occupants. The address may not be fictitious. However, without further surveillance, neither man could be sure that the house was safe to approach. Joe Fáinne and Sinn Féin could conceivably have set a trap for any unsuspecting, inexperienced police officer.

Scott and O'Brien stood on the opposite side of the street, Scott smoking his pipe and O'Brien casually striking up a conversation about the injustices of home rule — in an effort to blend into the community at large. Scott responded in like, feigning interest and their mutual disgust at the perceived British injustices of the executions following the arrests in the wake of the Easter Rising. He finished his sentence with an appropriately placed: "Up with De Valera!" And at that precise moment, two city policemen approached and appeared to be walking straight towards O'Brien and Scott in luminous curiosity. The two men averted their gaze, so as not to make eye contact with the approaching constables. Scott inhaled from his pipe, while O'Brien turned and started to walk across the street, so as not to appear as though the two were loitering. As the two constables reached Scott, they both paused for several seconds, standing idly on the pavement, eying Scott and seemingly sizing up his intentions.

The first constable focused on DI Scott suspiciously before the second constable addressed his colleague and suggested they stop at the local pub down the street for a drink before heading back to their station and signing out. The two constables moved off at a slow, steady pace. They occasionally glanced around the neighbourhood, and up and down some alleyways before moving off toward the city. When O'Brien perceived the immediate threat to be gone, he moved back across the street to join his Herculean companion. On seeing Scott and O'Brien, a couple of street urchins ran across to greet them with urges for some coffers. Scott beckoned the two boys to come closer. The two scruffy looking boys were no more than eight or nine years old and clearly wore clothes that were two sizes too big; their grubby, soot-covered, cherub-like faces slightly obscured by oversized, slanted, tweed caps. Scott addressed both of the boys, as O'Brien eagerly watched the house across the street.

"Lads, I'll give ya tuppence each if ya'll do as I say?"

The two boys looked at each other and eyed Scott quizzically. "Now, list'n boys, I'll giv' ya da money after ya do as I say. Ya see dhat grehn door ov'r dare — number terteen?" Scott pointed across the street at a badly worn green door. The two lads nodded in unison. "Ring dhat doorbell und dhen meet m' friend 'ere in aboot ten minutes at da corner dhune dare." Scott raised one enormous digit and pointed to the street corner slightly east of their current position.

The two scruffy boys scuttled off in a whirlwind of dust and landed on the doorstep of the tenement with the weathered green door within seconds. The smaller of the two boys, who was clearly the leader, stepped upon the doorstep and raised his stubby fist, jubilantly knocking three times and then ringing the doorbell. No sooner he was done, they whisked themselves off down the street and stopped abruptly at the corner Scott had designated. Scott motioned to O'Brien to pay the two boys while he waited to see if the green door opened.

O'Brien pulled a tuppence out of his jacket pocket and the two lads eyed the coin eagerly. O'Brien addressed them:

"List'n t'me boys! Go home und doncha be hangin' aroond 'ere anymore!" The two young boys sensed what was brewing and shot away on their spindly legs towards the city without as much as a thank you.

DI Scott watched the tenement, paying careful attention to the drab curtain-drawn windows for the slightest movement. As he kept his gaze on the tenement, suddenly two muffled gun shots rang out from the second floor. Scott immediately glanced down the street towards O'Brien, as O'Brien moved at double pace towards Scott. But DI Scott shook his head, motioning to O'Brien to remain where he was; instead, Scott strode towards O'Brien at a gallop. He stopped abruptly as he met O'Brien almost nose to nose.

"We're officers of da law, but we're 'ere to observe und we cannat reveal our true identities. We'll leave dis to da local law enforcement. Dis is beyond da boundaries of our jurisdiction." O'Brien reluctantly nodded and they stood their ground in cover of growing darkness. Shortly after the gun shots rang out, a darkly clothed figure emerged from the alleyway next to the tenement. The figure carried tightly rolled up papers in his hand and moved judiciously down the street.

"Quick! O'Brien, follow dhat man! I'll search da

tenement. We'll meet back at da Gresham hotel."

O'Brien jogged off in quick pursuit of the dark figure heading north towards the centre of Dublin. Scott dashed across the street and moved into the alleyway to gain access to the tenement as he heard neighbours calling the alarm. The door was slightly ajar, and Scott removed his firearm and entered the room. The door opened to a small kitchen, with a single table and four chairs tucked neatly underneath. A single cup of tea sat on the table and appeared recently poured. He moved from the kitchen to the other rooms, hastily searching the first floor before moving upstairs to the bedrooms. He entered the first bedroom and noticed the scent of gunpowder. Kicking the door open, he was greeted by a dark-haired, middle-aged gentleman lying awkwardly on his back on the floor. There were two gunshots direct to the man's temple and blood pooled around his head, seeping into the oak floor. Scott moved fast and searched the dead man's pockets. He removed the identification papers and searched the desk in the room, but finding nothing, Scott exited the tenement and headed north towards Dublin centre. As he moved down the street, he heard the sound of police whistles and several RIC constables approaching with thunderous boots clapping down the street towards the tenement. Scott removed his calabash and paused to light his pipe as two more constables flew past, whistles screeching as their footsteps quickly vanished up the street.

It was early evening before O'Brien returned to the Gresham Hotel and met Scott at the hotel bar. Sitting on the table in front of Scott were the dead man's identification papers. O'Brien sat down across the table from Scott.

"I woz beginning t' wurry aboot ya, O'Brien." Scott moved the identification papers across the table into O'Brien's view. "Barman! Bring m' friend 'ere a meejum[3] of Guinness." O'Brien picked up the papers and solemnly studied them.

"He wuz one of us!" whispered O'Brien.

"Yes," Scott responded. "Our Irish Republican Brothers 'ave been moving most expeditiously today…"

"I ran into several RIC patrols in the city and overheard that Collins' squad 'ave hit several undercover British intelligence agents[4]," added O'Brien. Scott gravely nodded in acknowledgment.

"Und I suspect dis murdered fella, a captain in the RIC, was one of doze agents. We can't git muddled into dis mess. Und I know dhat hangs heavy on our conscience, but dare are udders who are fighting dis battle." O'Brien sipped his Guinness and sat staring at the dead man's papers.

"I followed dhat suspect," declared O'Brien after several long minutes passed. "Und he met up widh a group of udder fellas at Café Cairo in Dublin. I couldn't git close enough to list'n into dare conversation. But it woz clear dayh were part of today's events und I suspect part of Collins' squad. I left before I was discovered."

"Tanks, ya did well, O'Brien. It's just as I taught. Dare's nothing we cunh do but fight one battle at a time."

"Ya tink dis 'as anyting t' do widh da Milling's murder?" quizzed O'Brien.

"I only know one ting fur sure lad… Dis new nationalist sentiment will bring much upheaval in Ireland before it's all said and duhne." Scott took another long sip of his meejum.

Just as O'Brien lifted his gaze from the dead man's

papers, he spotted two familiar looking men walking into the hotel lobby. O'Brien lowered his head and pulled his cap down to obscure his face and addressed Scott in a mere whisper.

"Dare are two men in da lobby. I recognize 'em from da fellas I saw in Café Cairo earlier today." Scott didn't move or say a word. Instead, he calmly rose and walked over to the bar. O'Brien continued to sip his meejum of Guinness[3] with his head still tilted slightly downward. The two men in the lobby took root in one spot and were facing each other, exchanging words. The taller of the two men, with a beard, spoke while the other, much shorter, stockier fellow listened intently, head slightly cocked. The stockier man had his back to the bar, while the other had a panoramic view of the bar room. Scott motioned to the barman and ordered another round of drinks, then turned his attention to the two strangers in the lobby. The taller of the two men had ceased talking now and appeared to be listening to the other speak. He had a noticeable scar on his left cheek and dark-brown, beady little eyes that scanned the lobby as people milled about and guests entered. He looked at his watch and returned his attention to the stocky man. As the bearded man shifted and turned, his open jacket moved enough for Scott to notice a revolver tucked neatly in the top of his pants. Suddenly, the two men strode purposefully towards the stairs leading to the upper floors of the Gresham.

Scott settled with the barkeeper and motioned to O'Brien to follow. O'Brien took one last gulp of his libation before taking three enormous paces that brought him to the lobby. Scott and O'Brien were on the first floor before the shots rang out and a series of short, punctuated caterwauls erupted from the second and third floors. They leapt up the remaining floors,

Scott moving swiftly towards the commotion outside the room on the second floor. O'Brien bounded up another flight of stairs to the shrill sounds of horror coming from a third-floor room. The scent of gunpowder hung oppressively in the air as Scott approached the guests gathered outside one room; one lady had apparently fainted in the hallway and was being attended by other guests attempting to revive her with smelling salts. Scott's imposing figure, along with his Webley drawn, cleared the hallway fast and the guests who had gathered in the doorway at the scene of the crime. He peered cautiously into the room and noting the all clear, identified himself as an RIC police officer and commanded the guests to return to their rooms until further notice. DI Scott assessed the room quickly, before other RIC officers arrived on scene. A single man lay dead, still wearing his striped, blue pyjamas. One gunshot directly to the head; the dead man was well-kept with a gentile and noble appearance. Scott moved to the man's jacket and searched for any identification papers: Captain McCormack[4], Royal Army Veterinary Corps. Scott returned the papers to the jacket and hastily exited the room.

O'Brien was standing in the room holding the second dead man's papers in his hand as Scott entered.

"Leonard Aidan Wilde[5]," announced O'Brien. "Doesn't appear to 'ave any military identification card on him."

"Let's go before our Dublin colleagues arrive with som' awkward questions we won't be able to answer!" Scott interjected.

"Aren't we gonna pursue doze murderers?" asked O'Brien.

"O'Brien, you've gotta stay focused on da end game. We

cunnat git caught up in dis trouble, not now, not dis way. Dis conspiracy to commit murder goes far deeper dhan two district RIC police officers, da likes of which cannot afford to handle at dis time… dare'll be time enuff for dhat, O'Brien. I promise ya!" O'Brien nodded pensively.

Scott and O'Brien returned to their rooms and hastily gathered their belongings, wasting no time departing. The aliases they had registered under ensured no awkward questioning after they departed Dublin and returned to Westport. As the two men headed south towards the train station, sounds of approaching officers' whistles could be heard. It seemed like the whole city was abuzz and bustling with agitated crowds and outbursts of whistles from every quarter. Riot police squads could be heard marching on foot from various sections of the city, distant streets aglow as rioters threw Molotov cocktails at squads of riot police in brief skirmishes. As Scott and O'Brien crossed the Liffey Bridge, two men in suits approached from the opposite end. The two men were nondescript and of average build and height. They looked more relaxed than they had reason to be amid the ensuing chaos. Both Scott and O'Brien took note of this. The taller man with dark brown hair had a slight limp as he ambulated forward almost crab-like.

Scott nudged O'Brien as the men moved closer. "O'Brien," Scott murmured, "Da man widh da limp… he looks familiar. But I cunnat fo' da life of me place him." O'Brien simply nodded as they inched closer to the other end of the bridge. As the gap closed and they were merely yards apart, the two strangers eyed Scott and O'Brien suspiciously. The taller man with the limp whispered something into his companion's ear. The strangers moved past Scott and O'Brien like predators ready to pounce at the slightest provocation. Likewise, Scott and O'Brien moved steadily forward without as much as a blink of an eye; their hands at the ready to remove their pistols. When they reached a safe distance from their counterparts, Scott turned his attention to his companion.

"I swear I know dhat face!" announced Scott. "But from where?"

"I'm sure it'll come to ya soon, sir," replied O'Brien.

"Oh, und by da way, O'Brien..." Scott paused in contemplation for a brief second. "Dhat man widh da limp... Did ya notice da trail of blood?" O'Brien turned to his companion in surprise, but continued walking without missing a step. "Und if ya noticed both men had about 'em a distinct smell of recently discharged gunpowder mixed widh whiskey. But did ya notice the scent of whiskey was not from dare breathe but radher dare clothes!"

"Dare clothes?!" exclaimed O'Brien.

"Yeh, dare clothes! Why would dhat be, O'Brien? Dare's no doubt deez men are som' of the perpetrators o' t'night's events; Sinn Fein, no doubt," continued Scott.

"But why not apprehend 'em?" declared O'Brien.

"O'Brien, our paths will cross again som' day. Of dhat I'm certain," declared Scott emphatically. "Und we don't want t' reveal our hand too soon eiddah!! But let's tink aboot why deez two men had a scent of whiskey aboot dhem?"

O'Brien paused, and searched the distant Dublin horizon for an answer. "The Marrowbone Lane Distillery![6] Und it's not much faddah dhan a mile from 'ere!"

"Yes, O'Brien! We'll make a fine detective outta ya yet,

my lad!"

"Ya tink there's some connection with the Marrowbone distillery? enquired O'Brien."

"Yes, I tink O'Brien, dhat dare's more t' da Marrowbone Lane Distillery[7] dhan meets da eye!"

The train ride back to Westport felt like an eternity for both men. Scott gloomily gazed out the window at the passing scenery the entire time without muttering so much as a syllable. Clearly, he was in a deep contemplative state; a condition that O'Brien knew all too well never to interrupt. O'Brien had some burning questions that needed answers. About an hour and a half from Dublin as the train gradually pulled into Longford station, it was only then that Scott finally turned to O'Brien and, with a pensive expression announced, "O'Brien, quick as we cunh now, we should make our way to da police station." Scott offered no further explanation and quickly turned his gaze back to the world vanishing by beyond the confines of the carriage.

Scott and O'Brien eagerly awaited the carriage's arrival into Westport. They were among the first passengers to gather all their belongings and stand in eager anticipation at the carriage door awaiting to disembark. The train had yet to come to a complete standstill when Scott's size elevens hit the platform almost at a gallop, with O'Brien doggedly trying to keep pace behind.

The events of the night before in Dublin on November 21, 1920, were soon dubbed Bloody Sunday[7], making headline news, and revealed that thirty-one people had been killed. Fourteen British agents and police personnel; fourteen Irish civilians; and three Irish Republican prisoners were all reportedly among the fatalities. Scott pondered the events of the night before as he read the news; but slowly his attention returned to Joe Fáinne, the MacBride brothers and his nemesis – DCI Marlowe.

Chapter Eleven
Croagh Patrick

Scott now believed it was no coincidence that he and O'Brien had been drawn into the events of Bloody Sunday in the hopes that the two men's lives would have been brought to an abrupt end, swiftly followed by any further investigation into the Milling murder. He speculated at the magnitude of the conspiracy involving Milling's assassination. Scott lit his calabash, placing his feet upon the large oak desk, and inhaled deeply while he carefully pondered the connection between the MacBride brothers, Joe Fáinne and the likes of Marlowe. Could there be a possible connection between Joe Fáinne and Marlowe, and could Scott expose it?

Scott knew to be sure of anything, he needed to keep his wits about him and stay on course. In an indiscriminate and unbiased world, the investigating officer resides in, he must take a series of seemingly random events and piece them together to reveal the untarnished truth. This was the one and only incontrovertible constant Scott knew.

"O'Brien!" yelled Scott from across the tiny police station.

"Yes, sir!" responded O'Brien, poking his head up from a warm cup of tea.

"Bring me da Milling case files, would ya?" Scott sat up,

removing his enormous feet and ungainly Great Dane-like legs from the top of the desk to the wooden floor in one almighty wallop.

O'Brien hastened carrying a dozen, neatly stacked loose files in his arms.

"'ere ya go, sir! Deese are all the Milling files we 'ave."

Scott quickly buried his nose in the files, as O'Brien perched half on and half off the corner of his desk, waiting patiently for any crumb to be thrown in his direction, like an eager bloodhound waiting for a scent of its prey.

In a March 23, 1918, unlawful assembly and drilling deposition, with Joe Fáinne as one of the defendants, there also appeared several others, including one Jim Reilly. The name caught Scott's eye immediately. "Hmmmm, Jim Reilly!" thought Scott.

Scott lifted his gaze from the deposition and turned it to the summit of Croagh Patrick[1] known as the Reek by locals, hovering majestically amid some low cloud cover in the distance, somehow flirting and seemingly toying with Scott's searching mind. He was momentarily mesmerized and recalled his youth, climbing to the summit countless times with his father and Molly, their devoted and energetic red setter, where she was now laid to rest. It was during all those journeys to reach the summit that Scott had learned much about how to tackle life's energetic hills and valleys through his father's very astute and worldly eyes. Scott closed his eyes briefly and could hear his father's words cutting through the majestic silence just as clearly as if he were standing right next to him.

"Son, watch your footin' on dhat shale! It'll no sooner cut ya up, dhan shake ya 'and Rememb'r, just as in life, always be sure ya 'ave a solid footin' before proceeding up or down a mountainside."

Scott returned his focus to present day. The deposition concluded and all men had been remanded in custody for further sentencing in Castlebar at coercion court. Scott knew RM Milling chose his ruling carefully so as not to appear biased, particularly in the wake of Joe Fáinne's allegation that Milling had come to court with sentencing already decided upon for all the accused. But nothing could be further from the truth. Scott felt uneasy; a sign that perhaps he was getting closer to something that would eventually lead him to solving Milling's murder and uncovering a deeper conspiracy. He slowly moved from one file to the next, scouring each deposition tirelessly until the early hours of the morning. His fellow constables had long since retired to their beds. O'Brien had fallen asleep in a severely worn brown leather chair in the corner of the station. The faint glimmer from a solitary paraffin lamp flickered as shadows danced off the walls and a barn owl hooted in the distant night.

Scott was soon resolute in his next course of action. More legwork was needed to uncover further allegiances between the growing list of suspects and conspirators. The courthouse at Castlebar must be his next stop come daylight. The clock struck three a.m., and even Scott's unflappable single-mindedness started to fade. He walked over to where O'Brien was hunched fast asleep in a badly worn Ross & Co.[2] brown leather armchair and placed his large paw on O'Brien's shoulder, so as not to alarm him. "O'Brien!" O'Brien opened his eyes as signs of consciousness slowly flickered back.

"Git ya'self to bed, lad! We 'ave a busy day ahead of us in

Castlebar!"

"Castlebar?! Aye, DI Scott! Wot time we leaving?"

"Meet me at the train station at six forty-five a.m., OK?"

As the two men locked up the station and departed, sounds of foxes cried out through the still of the night. O'Brien and Scott soon reached diverging paths and the two men bid farewell.

Chapter Twelve
Castlebar

Located in the middle of County Mayo is Castlebar, the largest town in the county. The old courthouse was built in 1855 and stood with its hexastyle Greek Doric portico to the ground floor; the exterior austerity matched only by the echoes of occasional precise footsteps and the sound of resolute gavels upon a judge's bench. Scott and O'Brien proceeded directly to the courthouse records office. The two men didn't speak a word but for very different reasons. They moved scrupulously through the courthouse until they reached a small sign hanging above a solid oak door that read "*Records*".

O'Brien tentatively turned the handle and opened the door for Scott to make a dramatic entrance. Inside the records office there sat five women busy at work, most in their mid-forties, with the exception of one young lass, Millicent, who went by the name of Milly. Nineteen-year-old Milly Kilraine, the daughter of the Right Honourable Judge Kilraine who presided over afternoon sessions. It was no coincidence that Scott had brought young O'Brien to Castlebar; Milly and O'Brien had known each other since elementary school, long before Judge Kilraine had accepted his current position. Young Milly and O'Brien had grown fond of each other over the years, and it was this alliance that Judge Kilraine had taken exception to, when two years earlier he decided to move his family to Castelbar and accept the role of District Circuit Judge. Judge Kilraine was fiercely protective of young Milly and felt very strongly that the life as a wife of an RIC police officer was not apropos for Milly.

As the men entered the records office, young Milly's eyes instantly lit up. Scott noticed that O'Brien was no less moved. Milly sat perfectly straight, her posture second to none in a wooden chair behind a large oak desk covered in stacks of court documents and files. She wore a pale blue dress with a white lacy neckline; her mousy light-brown hair tied neatly back in a single ponytail. Her piercing green eyes hung over her soft, delicate, porcelain-like features. She wore no makeup, but her cheeks were obviously flushed.

The older of the women spoke first, "Good morning, gentlemen, and how cunh we 'b of assistance to ya?"

"Ah-hem!" Milly cleared her throat as she rose. "I know deese gentleman, und will be happy to help 'em." The older woman turned to face Milly, looking a little perturbed. But acknowledging Milly in the presence of the two men with a slight tilt of her head returned to her business. Milly sauntered over to the counter where Scott and O'Brien patiently awaited.

"Jimmy! Wot are ya doin' 'ere?" quizzed Milly, seeming to turn a rather deeper shade of crimson.

"Ahhh, I'm afraid dhat's my fault, miss," interjected Scott. "We 'ave some police bizniz to take care of, und young O'Brien drew da short straw und woz forced to accompany me to Castlebar. I hope dhat I haven't caused any trouble fo' ya, miss!" Milly simply nodded and smiled.

Milly adjusted her composure and cleared her throat.

"Hem... Und how may I help ya gentleman today?" Milly continued.

"We're 'ere to review some depositions from March 1918," declared O'Brien.

"I see, und do ya 'ave a case number in mind?"

"No," replied Scott. "But I cunh tell ya da defendants' names on da docket and date of da hearin' if dhat would help?"

"A-hem, well dhat'll certainly be a good place to start..." responded the fresh-faced lass.

Scott handed Milly a list of names he pulled from his coat pocket on a crumpled piece of torn brown paper. Milly studied the list after straightening out the badly crumpled paper and disappeared for what seemed like an eternity. When she finally returned, she had one large brown manila folder under her arm. She reached over the counter and handed it to DI Scott. O'Brien returned a smile and Milly looked flushed once again. She left the two men seated at a visitor's table so they might review the deposition and case files in peace.

"Hmmm..." pondered Scott.

"Wot is it, sir?"

"Look at dis, O'Brien!" Scott turned the court documents around so O'Brien could read them. Scott had clearly been looking for the person or persons who had posted bail for Joseph Fáinne. Young O'Brien's eyes widened as he scanned the court documents and landed upon the piece of information Scott had been seeking: *Arthur Griffith*!

"Aye, lad! I tink we've found wot we've bin lookin' fo', Constable O'Brien. Now, lemme give ya a friendly piece of advice... Go back in dare und ask dhat young lass out fur dinner tonight. We cunh stay in Castlebar tonight und return to

Westport tah-morrah."

O'Brien hadn't expected such generosity, and gleefully accepted without further ado.

"I dunno if dis is just city courage talkin', but I'm gonna do exactly dhat. If I'm not back in five minutes cumhe find m', coz Judge Kilraine will probably 'ave me detained and behind bars for da night." Scott cracked a brief smile.

"I'll be waitin' outside for ya," Scott added and turned, taking one expeditious leap toward the front of the courthouse.

The next morning came all too fast, but O'Brien could barely withhold his elation for the entire twenty-minute train ride from Castlebar to Westport. Scott noticed his colleague was giddy with a heightened sense of self-worth, rekindled by lost love. Scott himself was no less pleased with the outcome of the previous day's events. He had uncovered exactly what he had planned and was now armed with the most powerful tool in a law enforcer's repertoire: unequivocal factual evidence.

Scott spoke first, "M'tinks it's time we found Joseph Fáinne und 'ad a liddle word widh 'im ourselves, O'Brien."

"Und, how d'ya plan to track Mister Joseph Fáinne duhne?" responded O'Brien.

"I 'ave a feelin' dhat Mister Fáinne's gonna cuhme lookin' for us pretty soon, O'Brien. We just need t' be patient."

Upon their arrival at Westport police station, a court summons awaited Scott and his constables to appear in Castlebar. The summons citied DI Scott and his men as co-defendants in a wrongful arrest and detention case following Griffith's Sinn Fein rally at the MacBride farm several weeks earlier.

Chapter Thirteen
Seditious Act

Judge Kilraine wasn't happy to be presiding over a civil suit against the Crown, citing wrongful arrest and detainment of several Irish Republican Brotherhood plaintiffs versus DI Scott and his constables. Prior to the court proceedings, Judge Kilraine requested DI Scott conference with him in judge's chambers. Several members of the press had already descended upon Castlebar to report the outcome of the trial. Judge Kilraine feared reprisals and rioting in the streets of Castlebar if the final judgement wasn't met with approval by public opinion. And the wave of public opinion had definitely turned to the side of those supporting Sinn Fein, and an Irish Free State.

"DI Scott, I am at a loss 'ere," announced Judge Kilraine. "As a District Court Judge," he continued, "sworn to uphold the law and remain unbiased in deliberation, I am faced with da prospect dhat whatever da outcome of dis trial, dare is no winning proposition for da community at large, or fur doze dedicated to uphold da law. You and ya men's position 'ere seem wholly untenable."

There was a prolonged pause before Scott answered. "Ya honour, I do see dis trial places ya'self und da good people of Castlebar in a very tough predicament. Und yar right; dares no winning position 'ere. But ya know as well as I do, dhat dis is a frivolous trial, und a complete waste of time. Und I believe it's bin orchestrated by the Irish Republican Brotherhood in an effort to curtail me und my men's investigation into Charles Milling's assassination."

"Be dhat as it may, I've requested additional officers' und troops t' remain on call in case tings turn nasty once da trial is ov'r. List'n, Detective Inspect'r, wot happened t' Charles Milling was abhorrent and cowardly. To shoot a man in his own home in da back widh wife and child to bear witness, no less! 'Tis a cowardly act, make no mistake. I knew Charles Milling professionally speaking only; he was an honest, direct and likeable man. I wouldn't want to be in your shoes, DI Scott. You've taken on a very tough path ahead of ya. But know dis much, whateva support ya need along da way, I'll be happy to provide ya widh."

Scott briefly turned and stared out the window, before standing and addressing Judge Kilraine.

"I truly appreciate ya candor. As ya astutely noted, m' men und I are set upon a long und arduous path. Charles Milling woz a good, decent man; und he deserved more dhan da fate dhat awaited 'im, und his family."

"Good day, DI Scott! I'll be looking forward t'seeing ya und yar men in court dis afternoon."

The weather suddenly turned cold with a strong breeze entering from the east, with dark grey clouds precipitously dotting the horizon. As Scott reached the front steps of the courthouse, he noticed O'Brien and Milly in heated conversation in the street. Although Scott was not within earshot of the two, he could clearly see that Milly was agitated.

He bounded down the courthouse steps like a gazelle, taking two to three gigantic bounds until he reached the couple. Scott looked quizzically at them.

"Milly! You must tell DI Scott wot ya just told me."

"I don't want any trouble for m'father, Jimmy," replied Milly.

O'Brien shook his head and continued, "Milly, dis could be a matter of life und death. Ya dunno da likes of da people yah dealing widh; ya father could be in danger too. Ya must tell DI Scott wot y' overheard last night."

Milly broke her silence upon turning to Scott's immense and towering figure.

"I knew I shouldn't 'ave said a word!"

"Milly, dis is not a game we're playin' 'ere! You must tell DI Scott everything ya know!"

It wasn't shrewd to ignore Scott's overpowering presence. Milly acquiesced and recounted how she had woken from a deep slumber to voices of two men addressing her father in the drawing room downstairs the night before. She described how she had climbed out of bed as the voices grew louder and seemed more agitated; it was then she heard her father becoming increasingly more frenetic. Since Milly feared discovery, she didn't dare venture downstairs, but rather crouched at the top of the staircase while attempting to listen in on the conversation. It was a little after eleven thirty p.m., and as far as she knew her father wasn't expecting any company. She could only discern the identity of one man, whom her father addressed simply as Marlowe.

"District Chief Inspect'r Marlowe!" announced Scott. "Und ya didn't git da name of da udder fella?"

"No," answered Milly. "But…" Milly paused, "I did catch a glimpse of 'im when they left da hous'. Da udder man looked like a banker, well-dressed in a suit, dark hair, glasses and piercing brown eyes."

"De Valera! Did ya hear 'im speak? Und would ya recognize 'im if ya saw a photograph?"

"Yah, I'm certain of it," added Milly. "He had a very nasally accent, like he was from furthda south."

"De Valera was raised in County Limerick! By gawd! Und they do 'ave a nasally dialect in Limerick fo' sure, lass! You und O'Brien make som' fine detectives!"

Milly continued her account of the previous night's clandestine meeting. Marlowe and De Valera attempted to blackmail Judge Kilraine by first offering him greater prosperity, and then by claiming they could ensure the safety of his family when any troubles broke out. Kilraine wasn't having any of it; in fact, he sent the two men packing, and warned them if they returned or ever graced his presence again, he would have them both hauled off in chains to face bribery charges.

"Dhat's good, Milly, you've duhne us well. At least we know who we cunh trust. Und our friends from da Irish Republican Brotherhood are slowly leadin' us closer to our quarry!"

The afternoon's court proceedings were pure torture for Scott and his men. During frequent breaks, Scott paced up and down the courthouse while his constables all sat neatly to attention on the wood benches outside Judge Kilraine's courtroom. The only constable who was noticeably absent was the young upstart Reilly. Scott had ensured Reilly remained in Westport to man the police station while they were away. At close of day, the Crown had only heard half of the plaintiffs' testimony. Judge Kilraine called an end to the proceedings for the day and Scott and his men sought lodgings for the night. Watching Scott's nervous energy was reminiscent of a captive lion pacing to and fro in a cage. He was not a patient man when it came to obstacles that prevented him from pursuing a lead investigation of this magnitude.

"Magnum opus, O'Brien! Magnum opus!" declared Scott, as he led his men to the courthouse the following morning.

"Sir?!" quizzed O'Brien.

"Comes from Latin, meaning a 'great work', O'Brien. Dis is dare magnum opus! Ours is yet to cumhe!"

As the men approached the courthouse, they were met by a growing number of Irish Republican Brotherhood members, circling the courthouse steps, chanting and holding handwritten placards that read: *De Valera!* and *Free Ireland from British Oppression!* Scott had already briefed his constables not to incite any unrest intentionally or unintentionally among the protestors no matter what they said or did.

Judge Kilraine brought the court to order at exactly nine a.m. after all twelve members of the jury were seated. The jurors appeared to be a diverse group in age and gender, Judge Kilraine having insisted the jurors were selected not just from Castlebar, but from surrounding districts so as to ensure even greater socio-economic diversity. And sitting in the defendant's dock was none other than Arthur Griffith along with the local Sinn Fein leaders. Seated directly behind

Griffith was Maud Gonne dressed in her typical solemn dark dress and peacock-feathered hat. Maud studied and surveyed the faces of the jury meticulously, as if sizing each member up individually. The courthouse clock struck noon as the Crown prosecutors delivered their closing arguments for the plaintiffs. Counsel for the plaintiffs claimed the assembly had not been illegal, but rather a small gathering on the MacBride farm — on private property — to discuss the future crop rotation; this was the crux of their argument, citing the Seditious Meetings Act of 1817 that forbade all gatherings of more than fifty people called "for the purpose... of deliberating upon any grievance, in church or state". Counsel for the plaintiffs submitted evidence from DI Scott, the night of the arrests, and a handwritten list of those in attendance collected by Scott's own constables. Judge Kilraine admitted the evidence, and the jurors reviewed the list; it was duly noted that the total count was merely forty-eight.

Counsel for the defendants vehemently objected to this admission of evidence since they had not been privy to the document at discovery. Kilraine overruled counsel's objection and beckoned both counsellors to his bench for a conference.

"List'n carefully, counsel," Kilraine stared sternly over his glasses, peering down at the two men from high above on his bench. "I don't know wot games you're both playing 'ere; but m' courtroom is not a child's nursery in which you two can half-heartedly ignore the rule of law. Now git back to work and stop your shenanigans." Both counsellors turned like two chastised school children and promptly returned to their seats.

Counsel for the plaintiffs reviewed his notes, adjusted his jacket and waistcoat and stood up again to address the court once more.

"Furdharmore, section c.19 of da Seditious Meetings Act of 1817 requires all 'public' meetings to be summoned by an authorized official, and sufficient notice provided by its organizers." Counsel was now addressing the jurors. "No such documentation or public notice woz ev'r made. Deese arrests were nothin' more dhan local law enforcement grossly overstepping dare mark t' harass an otherwise lawful gathering of farmers concerned only about da well-being of dare crops." Counsel paused for several moments to ensure this last detail was fully absorbed by all jurors, before returning to his seat.

Counsel for the defendants stood, acknowledged his adversary with a slight nod and began his counterargument. "Ya saw dhat the total count of doze in attendance on da night in question woz listed as fordee-eight. Widh dhat in mind, I'd like to call one Henry Desmond Shields to the stand."

Young Henry Desmond Shields had been waiting patiently in the courtroom, listening intently to the proceedings, and expeditiously jumped to his feet upon hearing his name. Once seated, Judge Kilraine swore in young Henry Desmond, and counsel continued his examination of the witness.

"Ya are one Henry Desmond Shields, of 42 Mill Road, Westport?" the counsellor asked.

"Yes, sir, I ham."

"Und where were ya on da night of March 31st, nineteen-hundred and nineteen in the year of our lord?"

"I was at the MacBride farm," answered Henry Desmond. The jurors' attention suddenly zeroed in on young Henry Desmond.

"Und, tell me where exactly ya were on da MacBride farm on the night in question?" continued the counsel.

"I woz in da barn attending da Irish Republican Brotherhood meeting," responded Henry Desmond. Henry's statement was greeted by some gasps from the audience and jurors.

Counsel for the plaintiffs objected to Henry Desmond's statement. But Judge Kilraine hastily overruled the objection.

"Henry Desmond... und how cunh ya be sure dis meeting was held by da Irish Republican Brotherhood?"

"Coz, I saw Arthur Griffith!" Some of the jurors turned to look disapprovingly at one another.

"Und so, by my count, dhat would make forty-nine people in attendance."

Judge Kilraine piped in, "Where are ya heading widh dis, counsellor?"

"Bear widh me, ya honour; I'll git right to da point," he continued. "Young Henry Desmond brings our attendance up to fordee-nine, but we still 'ave two unaccounted individuals," he announced. "Doze two remaining men were processed separately at Westport police station by DI Scott's constables becoz dhey were carrying shotguns widhout a certificate." The counsellor suddenly looked very pleased with himself. "Und dhat, by my count, brings our number of attendees' fur da night to a grand total fiddee-one!"

The court erupted into a mix of jeers and claps from the opposing sides gathered in the courtroom. "Clearly, ya 'ave heard Henry Desmond Shields' testimony dhat also in attendance the night of March 31st, was nunhe udder dhan Arthur Griffith! Dis meeting woz obviously not one designed to discuss future crop rotations. Under the Seditious Meetings Act of 1817, I appeal to the court that all charges brought against DI Scott and 'is men be summarily dismissed." The plaintiffs' side of the court was now deathly silent, but their stillness was met with cheering and applause from Scott's supporters.

Judge Kilraine called for the court to come to order and addressed the jurors. He cited the merits of the opposing arguments and noted the jurors must take into consideration the Seditious Meetings Act, in particular section c.19 — all gatherings over fifty people must be publicly advertised in a newspaper with the time, place and purpose of the event, or submit a notice to a clerk of the peace. The advertisement or notice needed to be signed by seven local persons, and a copy was to be forwarded to a justice of the peace. These actions had not been followed by the organizers; moreover, evidence was shared that Arthur Griffith had been in attendance. Kilraine dismissed the jurors for deliberation, and added, "I expect ya deliberations t'be brief und we will hear from yar elected spokesperson shortly."

Chapter Fourteen
Fallen Comrade

During the previous day's court proceedings, Arthur Griffith had been whisked into and out of court by his entourage of Irish Republican Brothers so he could provide testimony. Judge Kilraine was adamant Griffith not sit in his court for the entire proceedings at the risk of inciting further public unrest at his presence. Scott bated Griffith, ensuring his counsel cross-examine Griffith and his known associates. Of particular interest was one Mister Joseph Fáinne. Scott succeeded twofold; first by bringing Joseph Fáinne back under the wings of justice, thus allowing Constable O'Brien to watch Fáinne once the court hearing was over; and secondly, to establish that Griffith and Fáinne were indelibly linked. Once the plaintiffs were duly processed and fines assessed, O'Brien set off to shadow Fáinne's every move. Scott's next target was an altogether different beast. He waited patiently, biding his time for the right moment and armed with more facts before he chose to tackle District Chief Inspector Marlowe. Marlowe had briefly appeared in court during the proceedings, feigning his support and interest in Scott and his men's welfare. But Marlowe surreptitiously retreated into the shadows once he had laid eyes on Griffith and his Irish Republican Brotherhood supporters. Scott noted the District Chief Inspector's very brief and curious presence.

Scott had sent all his constables back to Westport with the exception of O'Brien. O'Brien's mission was to track Fáinne's movements and report directly back to Scott. To that end, he had followed Fáinne to Chapel Street Lower where Jonny McHale's pub stood, one of Castlebar's oldest public houses famed for serving a meejum[1] of Guinness to its patrons. Castlebar was surrounded by smaller hamlets and farm land, with a grand tradition of open-air markets selling and auctioning livestock and locally grown produce. Today brought in a particularly busy trade in livestock and McHale's reaped the rewards of bustling wave after wave of farmers and farm hands. O'Brien concealed himself across the street but found it hard to resist walking into McHale's himself and ordering a meejum of Guinness within earshot of Fáinne and his pals. He knew better; Fáinne would certainly recognize O'Brien and the game would be up. He had promised Scott that he'd remain undetected. A hawk glided gracefully overheard in the thermals of the failing sun as a light odour of cow manure and hay was lifted by a sudden easterly breeze moving at a brisk pace towards Jonny McHale's.

Meanwhile, back at the courthouse, DI Scott had requested a meeting with Judge Kilraine. "Your honour, I tank ya for seeing me. I tink da trial had a satisfactory outcuhme, doncha tink?"

"I tink it's safe to say, tank gawd we'll be seeing da end to our Irish Republican Brudhas. I take it you'll be returning t' Westport soon enuff?" continued Kilraine.

"Ya, soon enuff ya honour; O'Brien und I 'ave a little police bizniz t' take care of first here in Castlebar."

"Ohhh? May I ask wot dhat biznis might be?" inquired Kilraine.

"Not wot, but who… a fella called Joseph Fáinne," answered Scott. "He's a key suspect in da Milling investigation."

"Ah… dhat unsavoury lout! I see, well dhen, gawd speed to ya und yar men." Scott nodded and promptly departed the Castelbar courthouse.

A single gunshot rang out in the vicinity of New Line and Chapel Street as a group of young men were seen running from the scene. Dusk seemed to settle in heavily. All that could be seen of the shadowy figures as they vanished into the night were silhouettes of three mid-sized men and the accelerated fading sound of their boots striking cobbled streets. O'Brien lay slouched against a brick wall behind McHale's with his chin propped against his chest. He had moved closer to the pub to try gathering more intelligence. As he turned the corner, he was greeted by three men exiting the rear of the pub, one of whom he knew instantly. He tried reaching for his revolver, but a single gunshot struck him directly in the heart. He was dead before he hit the ground.

A large group of mourners gathered at Aughaval cemetery in Westport on the morning of April 22nd. No clouds could be seen for miles around; and a solitary hawk flew overhead, wings extended as it glided through the thermals and searched the landscape below for prey. Scott appeared pale and haggard and withdrew himself from the other mourners, keeping his distance intentionally. Milly Kilraine consoled O'Brien's distraught, sobbing mother; Milly's arm wrapped tightly around her, as other close family and friends crowded the coffin and grave. The third funeral in less than three weeks had begun to take its toll on DI Scott. Scott was now left with five remaining officers under his command: Constables Patrick Hentschell; Connor Gormley; William Francis Frawley; George Walter Mills, and the mole, young Jimmy Reilly. The sobbing intensified as the coffin was slowly lowered into the depths of its earthy tomb. Scott glanced over at Mrs. O'Brien and young, innocent Milly. Her soft, porcelain white features appeared almost angelic; Scott's heart hung heavy to think what might have been between Milly and O'Brien. He carried an even more unfathomable grief, having lost another close friend, colleague and confidant. O'Brien was trustworthy and loyal to no end and he had had great aspirations for O'Brien's career.

As the coffin came to rest, the priest stepped up to speak: "*Accept this prayer which I offer You, merciful Father, for those who have died, those who have gone before us marked with the sign of faith, and those whose faith in this life was known to You alone. Have mercy on them all and bring them into Your kingdom of peace and light without end where You and Your saints live in the happiness which this world has not known and cannot give. Amen.*"

No sooner had the priest finished, ominous grey clouds coalesced upon the horizon as an easterly wind began to pick up from the coast. Constables Hentschell, Gormley, Mills, Frawley and Reilly raised their rifles and fired off three volleys. Scott could not be more resolute; he would find Joseph Fáinne and bring him to justice swiftly. There was now little doubt in his mind of who pulled the trigger that fatally wounded O'Brien and John Charles Milling. A county-wide manhunt would commence immediately until these murdering hoodlums were behind bars. But first, Scott would begin his advance en passant, on his nemesis in Castelbar.

Chapter Fifteen
DCI Marlowe

Returning to Castlebar the following day was not one of Scott's first choices of destinations. Nonetheless, he chose to enter the heart of the hornet's nest at whatever cost. Members of the Irish Republican Brotherhood had still lingered in town and were avidly protesting the outcome of the recent trial. Their continued presence increased Judge Kilraine's paranoia, and he had requested a stronger police presence around the courthouse until the rabble grew weary and dispatched themselves. Two constables under Marlowe's command had been seconded as personal bodyguards for Kilraine and his family. Judge Kilraine had been pleased that Milly had left town for O'Brien's funeral in Westport, if only temporarily. He had tried to convince Milly to go stay with her aunt in Dublin for a few weeks, but Milly steadfastly refused, a head strong and stubborn young lass who chose to remain by her father's side.

The weasel-like Deputy Chief Inspector Christian LaFleum greeted DI Scott as he entered the District Chief Inspector's office, as the two stood head-to-head, but Scott's immense physical presence dwarfed that of the weasel. One could imagine Scott's enormous paw swatting him like a common house fly into his desk. The weasel looked nervous and fidgeted; his tiny claw-like hands cusped as he rubbed them together in tiny circular motions.

"Lilly!" exclaimed the weasel, shouting over to the same young lass who greeted Scott on his last visit to Marlowe's office.

"Yes, sir?" she hastily replied.

"Fetch Detective Inspector Scott som'sing to drink."

"Yes, Detective Inspector Scott, wot cunh I git fo' ya? Som' tea?"

Without answering, Scott took his right paw and brushed LaFleum aside, and strode purposefully toward Marlowe's office.

The weasel feigned protest but was feverish at the thought of Scott's impending encounter with Marlowe. This wasn't a show the weasel intended to miss. Scott wasted no time; consciously choosing not to knock on Marlowe's door. The door burst open to Marlowe's surprise, as he sat squarely behind his desk, glasses perched upon his long, thin nose. DI Scott stared at Marlowe and turned to close the door.

"Wot's da meanin' of dis intrusion, Detective Inspector Scott?" Marlowe's mustache twitched ever so tellingly.

Scott pulled up a chair, sat down calmly, placed his elbows on the armrests, wove his fingers together and raised his hands to his face before judiciously choosing his opening statement.

"Dares one ting as an officer of da law dhat really vexes m' more dhan anyting else, Chief Inspector Marlowe. Cunh ya guess wot dhat might be?"

Marlowe's blood pressure was starting to rise, his face was getting visibly more flushed, and he wasn't about to take Scott's intrusion and abhorrent disrespect for his office and position lightly.

"List'n 'ere, DI Scott…" But before he could finish his sentence, Scott jumped up and was perched on the corner of Marlowe's desk within an instant.

"No, District Chief Inspect'r Marlowe," Scott continued. "Ya list'n 'ere, I taught long und 'ard about dis, und dares only one outcuhme dhat's remotely plausible fo' me…"

Marlowe's face turned a deep red hue as he began to protest at Scott's demeanour and vacant disrespect, but at that very moment the door swung open, and Judge Kilraine appeared in the doorway. The weasel, stood haplessly behind him, intrigued even more at the sudden commotion taking place in Marlowe's office. At that moment, Marlowe slouched back in his chair, as if finally succumbing to his fate.

"Tank ya fo' joining us, Judge Kilraine," continued Scott. "Und, as I woz say'n a moment ago, Marlowe, dares only one ting dhat I find utterly abhorrent as an officer of da law. Und I tink ya know wot dhat is!" Judge Kilraine approached Marlowe's desk and pulled up a chair. "Wot I don't quite know as yet, is how far-reaching dis conspiracy to commit murder is? Und why Charles Milling? He woz one of da finest men in law enforcement I know, und an outstanding und just resident magistrate County Mayo has never seen the likes of before."

Within seconds a single gunshot rang out in the room, one shot to his temple, the force of which was enough to send Marlowe and his chair to the floor as splinters of skull, brain matter and blood dashed the sides of the desk and adjacent wall. The second Marlowe drew his weapon, DI Scott had jumped from the desk in an attempt to intervene, but Marlowe was swift in administering his final act of justice. Gasps and screams quickly erupted from outside the office, as the weasel and the young secretary rushed to the aide of Scott and Kilraine to assist.

"He's guhne," announced Scott. "Dares notin' we cunh do fo' im."

"Well, da likes of dhat I've nev'r seen und hope nev'r t' bare witness t' agan," announced Kilraine.

The weasel hurriedly left to fetch a doctor and the local coroner. Scott sat in the chair next to Kilraine and raised his hands to his head in despair. "Widh Marlowe guhne, so too is m' lead to dis conspiracy theory. Dares only one more suspect who can lead m' to da truth."

"Wot about Griffith?" asked Kilraine.

"I wish dhat woz a solid lead fo' dis Milling investigation. But I can't touch da likes of Griffith, und I know better dhan to try; we'd all be buried in a legal battle widh 'is lawyers for all eternity," Scott replied. "We'd 'ave the entire Irish Republican Brotherhood descend upon Westport too! Dhay are an unenviable adversary, und I only 'ave so many constables to enforce the law, und I can't afford to lose more good men. Joe Fáinne is m' last hope of gettin' somewhere closer to da truth. A warrant for 'is arrest has bin issued, und time mus' surely be on our side now…"

Chapter Sixteen
The Unionists

The tumultuous political relations and sectarian violence between Ireland and England date as far back as the 12th century with the establishment of the Lordship of Ireland. Under the Lordship of Ireland, a system of feudal rule between 1177 and 1542 prevailed; the King of England became the Lord of Ireland. In 1542, the Crown of Ireland Act was passed by British and Irish parliaments. The Act set a precedent for a sovereign King of Ireland, which fell naturally to King Henry VIII. Over the centuries, when a Catholic King came to power, Protestants were subjugated and oppressed, and thus the cycle of oppression swung as one Protestant monarch was replaced with a Catholic monarch, and so rolled the fates of a King's subjects depending upon wherever the sovereign's theological pendulum happened to land.

Kilraine's family, like Milling's and Scott's, were Plymouth brethren, devout and loyal to one another, and to the Crown. The brethren often saw themselves as a network, or collection of overlapping networks, of like-minded independent churches. Perhaps it was this strong spiritual upbringing and structure that allowed for the most reliable and trustworthy of recruits for the Royal Irish Constabulary. For the brethren, there were only two viable vocations for their men: the army or law enforcement. The men of the Kilraine, Milling and Scott families all naturally gravitated to law enforcement.

Scott had long suspected the Kilraine's were Plymouth brethren, but couldn't be absolutely sure until Judge Kilraine came walking into Marlowe's office. It was only at that point that Scott knew he had a trusted confidant, someone he might share the details of the Milling investigation with, someone he might be able to enlist as an ally. To any Nationalist, Scott, Milling and Kilraine were considered Unionists, and proud of their deep-seated roots with Great Britain. Nationalists had sought armed insurrection against anyone standing in the way of complete separation from England; however, Unionist or loyalist paramilitary groups eventually took to violence in response to the growing Nationalist sentiment. And so too the cycle of violence continued.

As the coroner and doctor arrived at Marlowe's office, Scott and Kilraine retired to a waiting area where they sat facing each other.

"When ya find dis hoodlum, Fáinne, would ya mind if I were present during da interrogation?" announced Kilraine.

"I suppose it wouldn't hurt, Judge, but may I ask for wot purpose?" queried Scott.

"Well, I 'ave a personal interest in list'ning. Although I was not well acquainted with John Charles Milling, I certainly knew young Jimmy O'Brien very well, since he and Milly were knee high to a grasshopper. Und, I can't but help feelin' som' culpability in dis 'hole affair."

"How so?" asked Scott.

"Well, it seems, perhaps, if I had not offered greater protestations aginst young O'Brien entering the police force, he might yet still be 'ere today. He did look up to me, somewhat as a surrogate fadha. Ya know 'is own fadha was not quite da parental type, if ya know wot I mean."

"I'll 'ave one of my men call upon ya as soon as we 'ave Fáinne in custody," agreed Scott.

"I'd appreciate dhat, tank-ya."

Just then, the doctor and coroner walked out of Marlowe's office followed by two assistants carrying Marlowe's lifeless body on a stretcher covered by a white sheet, the sheet already absorbing blood at the exit wound draped over his head.

Chapter Seventeen
Scott's Eulogy

Young Milly Kilraine stood outside the Westport police station holding a bright red hooded cape over her head as a sudden spring shower passed. She looked forlorn, her eyes bloodshot, and was now partially drenched to the waist. Milly opened the door to the station and found Scott seated behind his desk, studying files and papers scattered haphazardly over each square inch as usual. Constable Gormley welcomed her, as Scott stood and beckoned her over. He offered her some tea, but she politely declined.

"Good afternoon, lass," smiled Scott. "Und wot cunh we do fo' ya?"

Milly returned a smile and pulled a letter from her cape pocket. "Dis woz intended fo' ya, Detective Inspector Scott." Milly handed over the letter. Scott noticed the envelope had been opened.

"I'm sorry, but I had to read it," apologized Milly.

"I see," replied Scott. He lifted the envelope flap and pulled out the letter and began to read.

March 19, 1919

Detective Inspector Scott,

If you are reading this, I must have fallen like so many of my fellow officers before me. With this fate, I could not leave this mortal world without expressing my innermost gratitude to you. Whatever the nature that sealed my fate might be, I wish for you to know how honoured I am to have served with you and have been mentored by a gentleman whom I hold second to none.

You have given me an opportunity to learn this craft that I have held so near and dear to my heart. The only other passion in life that equals this is that of my adoration and love for Milly.

I apologize for failing you both in the end. I appeal to you, to not take blame for my own demise. I have lived, loved, and I have shared a great friendship. Godspeed to you and my colleagues!

Your friend & confidant always,
Constable James Patrick O'Brien

Scott placed the letter on his desk and sat down; Milly saw his eyes tear up, but he blinked several times to conceal his emotions, an outward manifestation of weakness in his mind.

Scott cleared his throat, "I am most saddened by da loss of O'Brien. He woz an outstanding young man. Despite all 'is personal challenges he had to overcome in life, he showed great fortitude and conviction for all dhat woz just and right in da world, und 'ad great promise of becoming a fine detective som' dayh."

Milly walked around Scott's desk as Scott rose, and she extended both arms to embrace him; arms that barely reached around his giant torso. Scott delicately returned her embrace, albeit for a brief moment, before withdrawing his enormous paws for fear of crushing her. Large pools of tears rolled down her cheeks. She quickly wiped the tears away, said her goodbyes and departed just as suddenly as she had appeared. The spring shower had passed, and the skies soon opened to clear, endless blue heavens, with a slight breeze coming in from the east. Scott left the station shortly after, heading easterly towards Aughavale cemetery, several miles from the station. Constable Gormley offered him a ride in their one and only Ford Model A squad car, but he politely refused, claiming he needed some fresh air and a daily constitutional. He moved forward with his coat tails dancing in the wind as he forged onward. Appearing as resolute and determined as ever, he bounded over the paths leaving a whirlwind in his wake. He promised O'Brien a *magnum opus* of their own and despite Marlowe's sudden demise, Scott's determination to deliver on his promise to O'Brien now consumed his every pore.

An old stone wall surrounded Aughavale cemetery and the sounds of bleating sheep from the abutting farms carried over a light easterly breeze. Scott soon came upon O'Brien's grave, where he made the sign of the cross and uttered an old Gaelic blessing taught to him by his grandmother: *Ar dheas Dé go raibh a anam[1]*. He stood motionless for several minutes before reaching into his pocket and removing his old detective badge and placing it carefully on O'Brien's tombstone. Before turning to leave, he saluted O'Brien one last time. Scott moved onto his next target, swiftly trekking across the cemetery until he reached the grave site of John Charles Milling. Freshly laid roses sat on the grave, a sure sign that a loved one had recently visited. He wondered if Lilla Milling was in town calling on old friends. He returned his thoughts to John Charles, his closest friend and confidant, and perhaps for the first time felt a deep chasm open up in his heart. They shared a certain symbiotic relationship as if they had been twins; each at times completing the other's sentence or half-finished thought. Both men often sharing a chuckle in those memorable moments.

From his other coat pocket, Scott searched for an old photograph of two young, slim cadets in police uniforms at the Phoenix Park training depot. He deliberately positioned the photograph in such a precise manner against the tombstone and placed a loose rock in front to secure it.

"Maith thú![2]" murmured Scott, as he again saluted another fallen comrade before he rose and departed.

The spring equinox brought gradually longer days to Westport, and with it, great swathes of lavender-coloured crocuses popped up in gardens and in the lush green fields surrounding Aughavale cemetery. It was a time Scott most admired in nature; the beauty, rebirth, renewal and with it the promises of new beginnings. He contemplated life's changes while he walked back to the station, and his thoughts soon turned to Joe Fáinne and with that, Fáinne had now become Scott's one obsession in life.

Chapter Eighteen
Finding Fáinne

Joseph Fáinne was raised by his father in the working-class slums in the north-side of Dublin. Out of wedlock, Joe's mother gave birth at seventeen. They had discussed giving the child up for adoption with pressure from the mother's family and a local convent of nuns that could broker the adoption process. But soon after Joe's mother started to show, her relationship with the father began to wane. When Joe was born, the adoptive parents were ready to take custody, but Joe's father had second thoughts, mostly out of spite for the unwed mother. He decided to raise the child himself, while the mother moved to Westport to live with relatives where she convalesced, finally found work and eventually married the local butcher. This was not a favourable set of circumstances for the young Joe Fáinne. And the dye was cast for the future of the young boy.

Scott abruptly woke from a deep slumber in his favourite armchair at Westport Police Station. He glanced towards the clock, just as it struck twelve a.m. The sounds of the chimes pierced his groggy, heavy-laden head. As his eyes regained focus, a manila folder perched upon his lap dropped to the floor and a photograph slid out. The black and white photograph showed a group of men at what appeared to be an Irish Republican Brotherhood meeting. Scott recognized Arthur Griffith in the crowd. And someone had circled a face of a young woman in the foreground among the crowd of men with her arm around a young man about the same height and frame of Joe Fáinne. Scott's eyes narrowed as he looked closely at the young woman's face.

"By gawd!" Scott declared. "It's Maud Gonne! Ya stupid lout, Scott! It's bin right in front o' ya dis whole time! Maud Gonne!" Scott reached for the photograph and as he did so, noticed some writing scrawled on the back.

Scott — Maud Gonne! The link we are searching for.

The handwritten note was simply signed, *O'Brien*. Scott paused, momentarily overcome by an immensely heavy cloud that consumed him entirely. As he regained his composure, he rose from the great cavernous armchair and cast the photograph onto his desk. With a single Brobdingnagian leap he swooped across the station house, scooping up his hat and coat and swiftly exited the station.

Scott strode purposefully home with one singular thought: to track down Maud Gonne — this, he thought, would be his magnus opus. He reached his cold and unforgiving abode at 12:33 am. He took out his pocket watch and noted it was a mere six hours away from catching the morning train to Dublin. He hastily packed one small suit case, almost forgetting to throw in his shaving kit before collapsing into a giant mound on his enormous wrought-iron four-post bed.

The sun had barely risen by the time Scott had arrived at the train station. He purchased his Westport-Dublin return ticket from a surly older gentleman behind a counter. Moments later, as he sat in his carriage alone gazing aimlessly at the passing farmland disappearing from view, he contemplated how to proceed once in Dublin. He knew finding Maud wouldn't necessarily be the issue, but rather questioning her without her protestations — that would be the challenge. He wondered how best to proceed. There would be no doubt of her outward hostility toward any lawman representing the crown. Perhaps then, he might take a different tack. He made his way straight to the Hotel Gresham on O'Connell Street to secure a room before planning his next move. As he gazed out of his hotel room watching the street, he saw all manner of life passing below. He stood there — a solitary voyeur for several minutes taking in all walks of life. A couple of working men moved jauntily down the street after having just retired from a public house. And then an idea hatched. One question remained — would Maud recognize Scott from the Castlebar court proceedings last year? Grabbing a pocket full of loose change, he set off for the nearest Salvation Army store.

Scott emerged from the store having replaced his own fine clothes with those that appeared one size too small for him and in part quite thread-bare in places. He hadn't shaven this morning, and now looked altogether quite common and you might even say of questionable character. He was a brute of a man in finer clothes of the day but remove all manner of outward prosperity and grandeur and Scott could easily be construed as a labourer, or perhaps even a common criminal. As he moved among Dubliners down the busy O'Connell Street, he found the upper-class women and men deliberately avoided him by crossing the street, or they would move suddenly into a store front window to escape Scott's gigantic stride. Some gentlemen even went to great lengths to eye him up and down before moving aside for fear of being crushed by the oncoming brute. Temporarily stripped of his social standing, Scott still commanded an indisputable monolithic presence.

Thirty minutes later, Scott slowed his pace as he moved east down Inchicore Road toward his final destination on the boundary of Kilmainham Gaol. He stopped and leaned up against a stone wall, pulling his coat collar up about his face. Gathered outside Kilmainham Gaol was a group of young women holding up painted banners decrying the ruthlessness of the British authorities and mistreatment of those held with the walls of Kilmainham. Scott smiled and thought to himself, "This might well be your *Magnus opus*, O'Brien."

Standing in the midst of several protesters was a woman of Valkyrie stature, with long, flowing piercing auburn locks, thrown back at times by a brisk autumn wind. She was instantly recognizable. Maud thrust her banner toward the sky as the small group of women gathered around the front of Kilmainham Gaol and chanted cries of defiance. Scott straightened himself, cocked his workman's cap slightly off kilter and gathering his wits inched closer to the women. Soon he had come within a few feet of the group. Some of the women eyed him suspiciously, but soon turned their attention to the main cheerleader, Maud. She ceased chanting momentarily, while turning to study the object of her companions' consternation. Scott smiled and tipped his cap at Maud. She requited the smile and returned to her public dissent detecting nothing untoward. Maud's colleague Hannah

Moynihan[1] seemingly to lose concentration for a moment, shot an amorous gaze at Scott's sheer physical presence.

Hannah turned to Maud, "My, my... isn't he a biggun!" Maud duly chastised Hannah and nudged her forcefully back to their mission. But Hannah couldn't resist the occasional glance towards Scott, who was now perched upon a bench trying to look as harmless and inconspicuous as humanly possible for such a gargantuan figure.

"All is not lost! Dare may b' a less intrusive path forward dhat yields da same result," contemplated Scott, as he returned a smile in Hannah's general direction.

Just then a young lad appeared on the scene carrying a bundle of Evening Herald newspapers. The boy set up shop across the street from Kilmainham Gaol slinging the bundle of newspapers to the ground. As if to declare shop was now open. He then placed one oversized work boot awkwardly attached to his spindly ankle with trousers visibly two sizes too small upon the stack of papers and begun yelling:

"Evenin' 'erald! Get ya Evenin' 'erald 'ere!"

Scott stood up and reached into his pocket pulling out a handful of coins and moved towards the paperboy. As he approached, the paperboy grabbed one copy and prepared the exchange for one freshly minted halfpenny in Scott's gigantic paw. Scott stood there momentarily opening the paper feigning interest within its pages. His back now intentionally facing the protesting women.

"Thank-ya lad!" The boy nodded. "I'll give ya another two half pennies, if ya'd do m' a small favour?" Scott now had the boy's full attention. "If ya'd hand dis paper to the young lass ov'r dare? The one with the long black hair holding the banner to the da left o' me. Do ya see her?" He continued tilting his head to his left.

"Yah, I see her!" He extended a hand and Scott deposited two more shinny halfpennies into an eager grubby little hand.

"Just wait til I leave und dhen hand da paper t' her laddie." The boy eyed him suspiciously and simply nodded before continuing his customary ballyhoo. Scott returned the nod and bounded off in an easterly direction down Inchicore Road with a renewed sense of urgency and vigour. Now all he had to do was wait for his prey to enter his web.

Several days had passed and Scott had spent his mornings at the Café Cairo dressed in his usual labourer's garb and his afternoons at the Gresham Hotel in more appropriate clothing. To avoid any questioning from the staff he began entering and exiting the hotel from the rear service entrance where he grabbed some maintenance overalls that he threw over his shabbier clothing. He ate in his room, choosing not to leave but for the occasional daily jaunt down O'Connell Street and the local neighbourhood for some exercise and fresh air. He was not accustomed to spending so much time in the city and felt the walls of his hotel room closing in; the brief excursions only helping periodically to relieve him of a growing sense of claustrophobia. A week had passed and still no sign of his quarry. Perhaps, the newsboy hadn't given his note to Hannah. Maybe she was suspicious and decided not to take the bait. A renewed sense of nationalism in Dublin had made it difficult to know who you could trust any more. Nonetheless, Scott forged onward, believing his persistence would pay dividends eventually. One thing his many years of experience as a detective had shown him, was patience.

After another long weekend in Dublin, the hustle and bustle seemed finally to be weighing on Scott as he arose from his slumber, feeling a degree more agitated than usual. He donned his labourer's clothes yet again, placing his overalls on and exited the hotel by his normal path without attracting any unwanted attention. Monday morning was customarily busy at Café Cairo. And Scott had become a familiar face at the café among its staff. He ordered as he usually did, some tea but milk and sugar had become less commonplace due to the growing shortage of supplies. The tiny café was crowded, with few vacant tables. As Scott turned from the counter, his eyes met a woman sitting by herself in the corner. She was gazing languidly out the window sipping some tea. He smiled satisfactorily and approached the table. The woman turned in surprise at the sudden towering apparition standing over her.

"Well… I taught you'd never appear!" she declared.

"Ma'm, I've bin 'ere every mornin' since I saw you dhat dayh," returned Scott coyly.

The waitress interrupted, bringing Scott his tea with a single slice of bread with some jam.

"No butter available today, sir. The bloody British are stealing all our food from under us!" Added the waitress, before turning on her heels and shuffling off to serve the next customer.

"Well… isn't dhat da truth," smiled Scott. Hannah Moynihan was a young lass of about twenty-something with boundless green eyes set against a crop of long, flowing jet-black hair that set off her delicate, pale skin.

"I'm intrigued," said Hannah. "How does a man of ya stature afford to frequent Café Cairo? You're not an agent, ar' ya?"

"A British agent? Ha!" laughed Scott. "Not on ya lif' miss! Although, I was startin' to wonder if ya suspected I... was... well... an agent tryin' to pry som' information from ya," continued Scott.

"And if'n ya were mistah, I might add ya'd be a very sorry fella!"

"Da name's William, miss. William O'Leary. M' friends call m' Billy."

"Hannah Moynihan. Pleasure to finally meet ya, Billy." Hannah lifted her cup and daintily sipped her tea. "So, what's ya line of business, Mr. O'Leary?"

"Ya could call me a courier, Ma'm. I carry messages from one district to anudah."

"I see. The brotherhood?" continued Hannah.

"I cunnut sayh, miss," Scott smiled evasively.

"Can't? Or won't," persisted Hannah.

Scott changed the subject. "Woz dhat Maud Gonne widh ya at Kilmainham Gaol da udder dayh?"

"Ahhh, is dhat why ya gave me dhat note? Ya want to meet Maud Gonne, the famous actress and suffragette! List'n Billy, if'n dhat's wot dis is all aboot, we cunh say our goodbyes now!" Hannah started to get up, but Scott reached over the table and gently touched her hand.

"Miss, I didn't mean t' offend ya. Please sit. I'm not interested in Maud Gonne in the slightest. Und dhat's da god honest truth! I've heard meny lessah men may be interested in Maud Gonne. But she's not my type!" Hannah sat back down and smiled.

"Well Billy, ya still haven't answered m' question? Is it the brotherhood ya work fur or nut?"

"Miss Moynihan, like I said, if I tell ya, I'd 'ave t' shoot ya. Und dhat would sincerely make most unhappy!" Scott was still touching her hand with his immense mitt. Hannah smiled and half laughed.

"Very well dhen Billy. It woz a pleasure meeting ya! But I must leave now. I have an engagement I must get tah." Hannah rose and extended her tiny hand, to which Scott graciously reciprocated.

"Da pleasure woz all mine Miss Moynihan. Perhaps, if ya'd be so kind to meet 'ere tah-morrah, same time?"

"Tah-morrah? I tink tah-morrah may work."

"Very well dhen, have a wonderful evenin' Miss Moynihan." And with that brief exchange, Hannah departed.

Hannah had been well trained. She had given nothing away beyond her allegiance. No sooner Hannah had left, Scott got up and walked out – lingering momentarily in the doorway, watching the direction in which Hannah moved. He waited until she was out of sight and started his pursuit. He moved down Grafton Street ducking behind pedestrians every now and then to conceal himself, when Hannah appeared to stop, every once in a while, to look back to ensure no one was following her. Each time Scott matched Hannah's movements as she paused, he would take cover in a store front doorway, or turn and lean on a wall and wave at some passer-by. Hannah continued to move south towards St. Stephen's Green[2]. She reached the west side of St. Stephen's Green and stopped at number 123 and waited on the steps to the Royal College of Surgeons. Scott lingered just out of sight keeping one eye on Hannah while staying keenly aware of his surroundings and other pedestrians in the vicinity. Now would not be an auspicious time to meet Maud Gonne.

An eternity passed while Hannah stood outside the Royal College of Surgeons, but eventually the door creaked open and out stepped Maud Gonne in a long black dress, fur shawl and a black cloche hat. The two ladies greeted one another and set off at a brisk pace and entered a very articulated, energetic conversation. Scott was too far from earshot to hear even a single syllable but started at a safe distance his pursuit. His curiosity was peaked. What business would Maud Gonne have at the Royal College of Surgeons? The women now headed towards the north corner of the St. Stephen's Green along a very prestigious street lined with grand Georgian homes with their seemingly austere rigid symmetry that appeared to stand sentry.

Scott tracked Hannah and Maud for the next quarter of an hour as they moved northeast towards Trinity College. As the two women reached Nassau Street[3] they stopped briefly before crossing and entering a Georgian brick tenement, number 19. Scott pulled out a small notepad and jotted down the address. He paused in a contemplative trance for many minutes, before being jolted back to reality by the sudden sound of horses' hooves crashing down the cobbled street as a regiment of mounted Black and Tans[4] glided past. He resolved to wait patiently out of sight for any further movement into or out of the tenement. Two hours passed and still there was no activity. His eyes remained fixated on the house only taking his gaze away momentarily to scan east and west along the street. Then, after what seemed like an eon, a small group of young men appeared from the west moving as one mass down Nassau Street toward the thick brick tenement. As they reached the house and ascended the stone stairway the door cracked open, and they were greeted by Maud. From Scott's vantage point — still secluded, his eyes narrowed as he squinted and tried to get a clearer view of each man entering the house, but to no avail. Scott reached into his pocket and pulled out his watch — it was now a quarter past two. He noted the time and number of men in his notepad.

Scott's patience was waning, and he decided to risk moving closer to the tenement. Crossing the street and walking slowly towards the brick building he stopped only briefly to adjust his coat collar and pull his cap down over his eyes. Then the door to the tenement creaked opened and there were sounds of salutations at number 19. In an effort to remain undetected, without missing a beat, Scott ascended the stairs to the house next door and removed some loose pages from his notepad and deposited a blank piece of paper into the letterbox slot. He turned away from number 19, holding his pad and pen in his hand and feigned as though he was making a note. The young men descended the stairs in a jovial mood joking and jostling with each other.

"Jimmy! Patrick! How about a drink at Johnnie Fox's[5] before ya head home?" one of the younger men could be heard yelling. They left number 19 heading in a westerly direction from where they had first appeared towards the tramline station. Scott followed at a safe distance intent to gather as much information as he could.

Johnnie Fox's, located in the village of Glencullen was established in 1798 with its clean white stucco exterior sitting neatly at the intersection of Red House Road and R116. Fox's was rumoured to have hosted many a meeting with members of the Irish Republican Brotherhood, though Scott was not aware of this fact. He lingered outside and let the group of men board the Rathmines tram to Glencullen keeping out of their line of sight at a safe distance. Once they had boarded the tram and it departed, he moved promptly to the ticket counter to purchase his ticket.

Inside Johnnie Fox's there was an energetic fire blazing in the stone hearth that greeted Scott. His quarry were collectively seated around the fireplace with pints of Guinness running full and fast among the boys. The men were laughing and joking as Scott inched his way through the thong of men huddled close to the bar. He greeted some as he navigated around them and moved into the bar to order a drink.

"Evein', und wot may I git ya?" yelled the barman from across the counter.

"A meejum, please." The middle-aged, burly barman simply nodded and turned to remove a glass stacked on a shelf above him. Scott placed one shilling and five pence on the counter. As the barman returned with the full glass, Scott nodded and slid the coins across the counter. He took a deep gratifying sip and turned his attention to the Irish fiddler playing in the corner accompanied by three empty meejums sitting by his side. The fiddler flushing red, was playing a vigorous little ditty while some of the crowd were tapping their feet and loud, blusterous hurrahs were echoing off the room's walls. Despite the fiddle music, Scott was close enough to hear the young men — gradually increasing in volume as the black gold started to take its effect. They were soon quite oblivious to their surroundings or felt less restrained in their current milieu. Among their count was Paddy Daly, Liam Deasy, the brothers Archie and Patrick Doyle, Andy Cooney[6] and Eamon Duggan. Andy appeared the most vociferous of their number and yelled haughtily at his comrades as his glass quickly drained.

"Lads, I've bin tru a lot wid ya's... bastards all of ye!" shouted Andy. "Now, who's turn is it? Git me anuddah meejum! Patrick — ya bastard — Déan deifir[7]!"

Scott pivoted to his neighbour at the bar, laughing and adding, "Ahhh, to be young ageen!" The older man to Scott's left simply smiled and raised his glass. The afternoon slid forward at a doleful pace and Scott was becoming more wary of his present circumstances. He could tell as a new face in Johnnie Fox's that he was commanding the occasional glance from the regulars. He'd give it another thirty minutes and then he'd make his way back to the Gresham with or without further intelligence. It had turned out to be a more profitable day than he could ever have imagined.

Scott inched his way down the bar until he was within an arm's breadth of Andy Cooney. Scott calculated the risk and was content with the consequences. This was for O'Brien. Scott turned to face the bar and lifted his meejum of Guinness to his lips feigning ignorance of group gathered around the fireplace, now cajoling one another for another round.

"Andy, it's yur turn, is it nat?" cajoled Eamon.

"Ah! Git away width yuz Eamon, ya bastard! Tis Liam's

round next!"

Andy huddled closer to his neighbor, Archie Doyle and lowered his voice almost to a whisper. Scott tilted his head slightly, narrowing his eyes — surreptitiously attempting to overhear the exchange.

"Meet yuz all at Maud's tah-murrah at 6 o'clock, okay? Maud has someone she wants us to meet." Archie simply nodded and turned his gaze back to the fireplace. Scott turned back to the bar, his meejum of Guinness almost empty and met the glaring gaze of the burly barman's dark, emotionless eyes.

"Will ya be 'avin' anuddah one mister? Wot parts are ya from? I've never seen ya 'ere before?" The barman's eyes still glaring squarely into Scott's eyes.

"Ahh… nah… I'm done… I've come in from Westport, bin told I might find som' work in deese parts, ya know!"

The barman's eyes narrowed… "Und wot sorts of work are ya lookin' fur?"

"Ya cunnat too be fussy in deeze times, anyting dhat pays!" The barman abruptly turned away and continued cleaning glasses. Scott recognized he had clearly over-stayed his welcome and decided it time to head back to the Gresham Hotel before his ruse was up.

Chapter Nineteen
Rendezvous at Café Cairo

It was a bleak, dreary Dublin morning when Scott arrived at Café Cairo, half expecting Hannah Moynihan to have stood him up. He felt tense. A discernible degree of uneasiness, almost like the nerves of an actor about to take the stage. But there Hannah sat solitary at a table in the east corner of Café Cairo sipping a cup of tea. She looked quite endearing and vulnerable at that moment. Perhaps it was that vulnerability that attracted Scott. Hannah seemed lost in her thoughts as Scott approached. She was jolted back by Scott's presence casting a great shadow over her and half of the room.

"Ah! Mr. O'Leary, I taught for a second yuz had stood me up!" her coy smile peaking over her tea cup.

"Miss Moynihan, I assure ya — I would never do such a ting!" They continued several minutes of niceties before Hannah made a curious change in her line of inquiry.

"Billy, are yuz lookin' fur work?" inquired Hannah.

"Ahh… who's askin?" replied Scott coyly.

"I'm askin'. But if'n ya 'ave someting dhat pays ya better, dhat'll be the end of it."

Not wishing to reveal his artifice, Scott played along. "Und if yuz are askin' who might yuz be representin'?"

"Wot are ya doing tah-morrah, at 6 o'clock?" Hannah

announced boldly.

"Well Miss Moynihan, it all rests upon yuz."

"Don't take it so pursonal, would ya care to go ought?" smiled Hannah.

"Ahh… dare it tis! I'd luv ta!" smiled Scott.

"Alright dhen, end of discussion," replied Hannah without a hint of coquettish hesitation.

As the two parted company, Hannah leaned in, kissing Scott squarely on the cheek.

"Meet m' t'morrah evenin' dhen, 6 o'clock, number nineteen Nassau Street," were Hannah's parting words. Scott simply nodded but inside he was beaming.

He stood gazing as Hannah walked off and languidly vanished among the pedestrians on Grafton Street. On a steady stroll back to the Gresham, Scott reminded himself nothing good would come from this alliance. He knew exactly where Hannah stood, politically at least. Although, she was still young and impressionable. Perhaps she might be swayed by common sense and logic to change her allegiance? "No," thought Scott. "I must keep m' personal feelings outta dis!" His self-reflection spun back to O'Brien and young Milly. His thoughts turned again to what might have been between Milly and O'Brien. Was Scott destined to live out the rest of his days alone in Westport? Perhaps there were worse things in life? He could never imagine himself living in the city. Hannah was nothing more than a pleasant distraction brought on by the loneliness of a large impersonal city. And ultimately, if Hannah knew his true identity, she'd more than likely throw him to the wolves and never look back. Nonetheless, he had never felt this kind of adoration for a woman, next to his own mother.

Although this was an entirely different feeling. His stomach twisted and turned inside out because he already knew what the end game would be.

Hannah arrived at 19 Nassau Street as Maud briskly walked her little Yorkshire terrier.

"Wuzzo! Wuzzo! Come here m' little darling!" encouraged Maud pulling on the little terrier's lead. Hannah greeted Maud as the two women climbed the steps to number 19 and disappeared into the front drawing room. The room was well lit and bright light-green chintz wallpaper covered the four walls in a mesmerizingly inviting pattern. They both sat demurely on opposite sides of the room facing one another.

"So, Hannah... and wot did ya find ought about our Mr. O'Leary?"

"Seems like a fine fellah t'me. But wot would I know? I invited 'im to a rendezvous here tah-morrah night at 6 o'clock."

"Ahhh... and he accepted, dhen?" Maud replied, her interest peaked.

"He did! I asked 'im if he woz looking fur work."

"Ohh? And wot did he sayh?"

"He seems a wee bit reluctant to commit," continued Hannah.

Maud smiled, "Doncha say? Wot man ever wasn't?" Hannah smiled but offered nothing more. "D'ya tink our Mr. O'Leary is trustworthy?"

"Ya tink he could be workin' for the British? A spy?" answered Hannah.

"We can't be too careful deese dayhs Hannah! You are

young and still 'ave a lot to learn. I don't mean to be condescending, but we 'ave to be thorough. We cunh never be too karfle. Try and find out more about dis fellah tah-morrah… where he's from, wot he actually does fur work and where he lives? Dhat way, we'll 'ave som' of our close friends make inquiries about dis Mr. O'Leary. Just don't git too close to 'im, Hannah. Und doncha give 'im too much credence until we are sure about 'im."

"Aye, Maud. I'll be sure to keep m' sensitivities closely guarded," declared Hannah. Maud smiled and promptly changed topic.

"D' boys are comin' t'night. I'll need y'ur help setting up the drawing room fur da meeting."

Chapter Twenty
Agent Provocateur

As Scott returned to the Gresham, he formulated a plan to gain inside intelligence. He weighed the pros and cons until his mind began to turn in circles, swirling around like a merry-go-round until the lines of justice appeared to blur uneasily. But as he regained clarity from his psychological catharsis, his focus seemed sharper and instantly he knew there was only one path forward. Entering his hotel room, he changed his clothes, hastily scribbled a note on a plain piece of paper and strolled down to the telegram office in the lobby. He handed the telegraph operator the handwritten note along with one shiny silver shilling.

"Send dhis immediately, please!' nodded Scott towards the note.

"Right away, sir!"

Scott turned and moved towards the hotel lobby to find a chair large enough to carry his enormous frame. He sunk back and reclined into a luxurious red leather armchair and exhaled deeply, closing his eyes briefly. Reaching into his jacket pocket he removed his calabash and started to fill the chamber with tobacco. But he didn't light it. Instead, he rolled his head back and gazed upward at the ornate ceiling in the lobby where scantily clad cherubs painted on the ceiling were floating above ionic columns. Contemplating the suspended cherubs brought Scott back to his present strategy in the making.

"Like babes in the woods," Scott thought to himself.
"Sir, you have a response!" announced the telegraph operator handing Scott a freshly typed telegram. Scott nodded and accepted the Great Northern telegraph. He opened the telegram and read the printed text:

> *Will arrive in Dublin on the morning training. See you at the Gresham — M.*

It was only now that the deeply furrowed brow on Scott appeared to melt away. He raised his pipe and struck a match, holding it over the chamber, inhaling ever so slightly as tobacco glowed and he exhaled a cloud of pure, white smoke. "Our magnum opus will be born soon, O'Brien. 'Tis a long time comin'" thought Scott. "Und you will play a part in writing the final chapter, my dear friend."

Scott stood stoically on the train platform awaiting the 7:30am train from Westport. As the train came to a stretching halt with steam spewing from the engine the sounds of passengers and porters chatting, and yelling filled the air. When the train had stopped completely, the doors slowly swung open. Scott searched up and down the platform for sight of his newest operative. Then the carriage door directly in front of him was slung open by a porter standing outside and young woman wearing a lavender lace dress stepped down smiling in Scott's direction. The porter took her bag as she waved to Scott. Scott strode forward to the porter.

"I'll be taking the lady's bag now, tank-ya," Scott nodded toward the small leather suitcase in the porter's hand, as he dropped a shilling into the porter's left hand.

"Ahh, tank-ya, sir! Good day to you both!" responded the porter as he shuffled off towards another waiting passenger.

"Milly! 'Tis wonderful to see ya, agin! I cannat say how delighted I was to receive your telegram!"

"Sir, I would not want to be anywhere else. I want to bring deese criminals to justice, not just for dear Jimmy, but also fur Mr. Milling. What they've done is utterly reprehensible und cowardly."

"Und Judge Kilraine understands the risks?"

"He does. Und he wouldn't have it any udder way," added Milly.

"Dhen let's git back to the Gresham and discuss the strategy."

Chapter Twenty-One
Magnum Opus

A mere five minutes from six in the evening on Nassau Street, Scott and Milly arrived at number nineteen neatly dressed and resolute upon their fate. Scott led the way up the stairs to the front door. Upon reaching the top step he turned and smiled reassuringly at Milly. The young lass moved to the step above and joined him. They both nodded at one another before Scott reached out one enormous fist and thrashed the door knocker three prodigious times. As he struck the door, Milly noted that the whole house seemed to quake under his fist. A short interval passed before Scott and Milly heard footsteps moving toward the front door on the wood parquet flooring amid faint voices and a woman's distinct but muted laughter. Though muffled, Scott lingered on the woman's amusement listening intently as the footsteps came to a sudden halt and the door latches began to turn and clunk. The green wooden door opened swiftly inward, and Maud Gonne's white face appeared like an apparition from some distant hazy dream.

"Well, Mr. O'Leary…" Maud paused as she scanned the woman standing beside him. "And you've brought a friend, I cunh see… To what do we owe dhis pleasure?" continued Maud.

"Ms Gonne, 'tis a pleasure to finally meet ya! I must

apologize for my unannounced guest. My dearest sister Milly Mae has just come into town, and I taught she would be welcomed. Considering Milly's bin a staunch supporter of da Irish Republican Brotherhood from da start."

"Ahh... dhen I welcome yar sistah, Mr. O'Leary!" Maud's eyes narrowed as she took in Milly for a few solid seconds before beckoning them both into the drawing room.

"Hannah, Mr. O'Leary... and dis is his sistah... Milly." Maud seemed a little uneasy. "Are you married Milly Mae?" enquired Maud.

"Ahh no," Milly responded clearly from the bottom of her throat. "I'm dreadfully single," she added.

"No apologies needed Milly Mae. A woman's worth should *not* be bound by matrimony alone!" Maud declared.

"Ah... no truer words have ever been spoken!" interjected Scott. "

"Well, Mr. O'Leary, yar full of surprises, aren't ya?" noted Hannah as she rose to greet Milly. The two women met dead center of the drawing room and gracefully shook one another's hands. Maud motioned for Scott and Milly to take a seat.

"Our udder visitors will arrive shortly," announced Maud, as she moved to take a seat in an armchair. "Mr. O'Leary, do tell what brought ya to Dublin?" inquired Maud.

Scott smiled. "A friend of mine suggested Dublin for work. Not much work in Westport deese dayhs."

"Is it the brotherhood ya working fur, Mr. O'Leary?" pressed Maud.

"Da *brotherhood*? Hmmm, I wish I could sayh. To be honest widh ya, I don't rightly know," continued Scott. Maud appeared content with Scott's answer, but still cast a look of suspicion in his general direction.

"Und Milly, what brings ya to Dublin? Just visiting yar dear brudah, no doubt?" Maud probed further. Milly sat up straight and looked squarely into Maud's eyes without batting an eyelid.

"Why yes, I taught perhaps I should cumhe see m'poor brudah. I hear the big city has a way of corrupting impressionable, young men," grinned Milly toward Scott. Maud and Hannah each released a slight smirk before politely restraining themselves.

"I cunh see how ya might tink such a ting!" smiled Maud, quickly changing the subjected.

"Mr. O'Leary, I'm curious... how do ya feel about da latest Fourth Home Rule bill?"

"Dare's not much to feel about it, is dare? Seems like we've bin down dis road befor'" responded Scott. "I would say dhat da British government is seeking ways to appease the Irish nationalists, particularly in the wake of the Easter Rising und the executions dhat followed."

Maud nodded approvingly and turned to smile at Hannah, who was now perched upon the edge of the sofa, listening admiringly to Scott's words. Just as Hannah turned to smile at Milly, three deafening knocks echoed through the house. Maud jumped up.

"Seems our udder visitors hav' finally arrived! Muttered Maud. "Hannah, please show our friends into the dining room."

Huddled around a grand Georgian dining table and chairs, Hannah, Milly and Scott waited patiently on one side of the elegant mahogany table. Soon Maud entered the room, trailed by five young men, ranging in height, build and aged from their early to late twenties. Scott closely observed each as they entered, taking mental notes of their clothing, physical characteristics and general demeanour, but most importantly their shoes — paying particular attention to any tell-tale marks that might reveal areas of the city they had recently visited, revealing signs of mud, soils, coal dust or wet and stained leather.

Maud spoke first. "Besides m'self — whom we all know… remember, we use first names only! Doze are da rules! Don't be breaking da house rules, und we won't hav' t' break yar legs!" Maud smiled maliciously. "I'll do the introductions, lads… please take a seat." Maud continued speaking, but Scott was still mentally cataloguing the most remarkable characteristics of the five young men now seated a mere arm's length away. Once everyone was settled, Maud stood at the head of the table and began.

"Glad you could all make it today boys… today we have some new friends who've joined our cause for justice and equality." Maud took a long deep breath before continuing. "Let me introduce Billy and his sistah Milly. Billy is an acquaintance of Hannah's. Und Milly is visiting her dear bruddah from Westport." Milly and Scott both nodded at the five men seated across.

Andy Cooney's eyes narrowed as he closely inspected Scott and Milly's faces before he spoke.

"Und how do we know we cunhe trust dem?"

Well, I'm so happy ya asked Andy, m' ever vigilant friend! 'Tis a simple proposition, really. We give them a task und we

see where dhat takes us. Now, Andy, wotcha say to dhat?"
Andy still eyed them suspiciously but acquiesced grudgingly.

"Und wot do ya 'ave in mind?" continued Andy.

"Well now, 'tis annudah excellent question. It's recently bin brought to m' attention dhat we 'ave more British intelligence agents working amongst us. Und, we happen t' know where doze agents meet on a regular basis. Billy and his sistah 'ere cunhe be our eyes and ears."

Milly glanced quickly at Scott, but Scott's eyes were fixated firmly on Andy Cooney. After a long pause Scott finally broke his gaze and addressed Maud.

"Maud, I know of da the place yar speaking of. I've heard from mutual friends. You want m' sistah und I to spy on deese men? "

"Dhat, Billy, will be your first task. You will meet Andy 'ere at a designated place und time each week for da next month with any information you gather. No need fur m' to tell ya to use extreme caution. Deese men are trained spies. They'll be covering dare tracks und will always be watching, ensuring dare not being follow'd."

"Aye, we'll be vigilant." He turned to Milly and smiled.

Milly cleared her throat and watched Maud sitting at the head of the table. Andy Cooney motioned to Maud to leave the room for a private conference. Maud stood and they exited the dining-room, moving into the hallway. All was suddenly quiet in the dining-room as the group across from Scott and Milly eyed them cautiously. Muffled, heated exchanges between Maud and Andy could be heard coming from the hallway. A long five minutes passed before the door opened slowly and in walked Maud followed by a sour-faced Andy. Maud appeared calm but stiff, and Andy's face was slightly flushed, as if he'd just sprinted up a flight of stairs.

Maud straightened herself and sat back down. "Now dhen, Billy and Milly will leave shortly und report back to Hannah as soon as they have some intelligence to share. The lads and I have som' more timely business to discuss in private. Hannah, please show our friends to da door. Billy, we will hear from ya soon, I trust." Scott merely nodded as he and Milly were led out the room by Hannah. Moving past a table in the hallway Scott noticed a recruitment poster for the French Foreign Legion.

"I don't tink Andy much cares fur us, does he?" commented Scott as they reached the front door, his eyes still fixated on the recruitment poster.

"Ahhh doncha worry about Andy. He'll git ov'r woteva ails 'im soon enuff, Ya 'ave t' earn Andy's trust. Und I'm sure ya will," added Hannah.

Milly smiled, "Hannah, might ya know a fella by da name of Joe Fáinne?" enquired Milly.

"Joe Fáinne? The name isn't familiar. Is he a friend of yours?"

"A mutual friend asked m' t' look 'im up when I was in Dublin. I just taught ya might know 'im."

"We 'ave a lot of fellas in the brotherhood that come and go through Dublin. Dare's a fair chance he's still in town. I cunh ask around fur ya," smiled Hannah. Scott feigned disinterest as he peered up and down Nassau Street, as if to check they weren't being watched.

"We'll be in touch, when we 'ave som'sing t' share," announced Scott as he descended the steps in two short bounds. Milly following with greater caution as Hannah waved goodbye and vanished behind the closing door.

Darkness had descended on Nassau Street as Scott and Milly headed in a westerly direction; the street only lit by solitary gas lamps lining the shadowy pavement. Pausing at the corner of Nassau and Grafton, an evening mist moved in to blanket them.

The likes of John Devoy[1] may have begun the trend, but Crown intelligence had long known the French Foreign Legion was a solid recruiting ground for Fenians[2] seeking to disappear from Ireland. The legion was a palatable arena for those escaping the law and train as a soldier and gain experience in warfare with an eye to returning to Ireland and continuing their fight for independence. Devoy had trained many a foot soldier in the Irish Republican Brotherhood after having spent a year in the legion fighting in Algeria. The Cairo Gang — the group of British intelligence agents working in Dublin had been sent there specifically to undermine this recruitment initiative. And it had seemed they had gotten close to their goal, judging by how swiftly the brotherhood had targeted the men and wiped them clean off the streets in one sweeping afternoon bloodbath. But Scott knew where one team *was* active, another would surely be waiting patiently in the shadows to take over from their fallen comrades. He just needed this second team to show their heads so he could provide a nugget of actionable information and gain an equal seat at the table with Andy Cooney. Scott moved doggedly through the intelligence cycle from planning and direction to collection and processing with the analysis and dissemination to eventually follow. Yet Scott knew, where the science behind intelligence gathering fell short, blind luck often provided the clues he so eagerly sought.

In the weeks to follow, Milly and Hannah had struck up a close friendship and Scott was pleased to have some inside information on Maud and her boys' plans. On one such rendezvous at Café Cairo, as Milly and Hannah sat and sipped tea vivaciously chatting away about life in Dublin, a young, suited fellow strolled up to the counter and ordered some soda bread. Supplies were limited, but if you got to the café early you might be lucky enough to grab a small piece of respite from the impinging food rations.

"'ello Mr. Fáinne," smiled the young lass behind the counter.

"Ah… 'ello Jessie," the man looked nervous, and uneasily turned around to see who was within earshot.

"I'll take som' soda bread dis mornin', Jessie. I cunnat talk t'day, I've gotta catch the train to Westport."

Milly noticed the nervousness in the young man but kept her head down concealing her face as she took another sip of tea. The man turned back to the counter, placing a handful of coins in Jessie's palm in exchange for the soda bread.

"'ave a safe journey, Mr. Fáinne!"

'Aye, I hope to see ya when I return!" He moved quickly out the door and disappeared before Milly could say her farewells to Hannah. She moved as fast as her feet would carry her back to the Gresham. Barrelling through the door as Scott responded to their predetermined coded knocks at his hotel room door. As she burst into Scott's room, he tried to calm her down.

156

"Whoaaa lass! Wot's got ya all worked up so early in da dayh?"

"I w... I woz... I woz...' puffed Milly, trying earnestly to get her words out.

"Calm down Milly, 'ere take a seat," Scott grabbed a chair and motioned to Milly.

"I woz just at Café Cairo meeting Hannah... wh... wh... when a young fella came in... da young lass serving 'im ad... ad-dressed him... as Mr. Fáinne!" Scott's eyes widened.

"Did ya follow 'im?" interjected Scott, his eyes lighting up.

"No, I couldn't beg my leave from Hannah widhout drawin' any suspicion. By the time I got t' da street he woz long guhn."

"It's okay, Milly... ya did ya best," Scott consoled her and placed his hand on her shoulder tenderly.

"But... I overheard 'im sayn' he was taking da train to Westport t'day!'

"Ahhh! Excellent Milly! I could kiss ya! Dis is grand news! Did he say anything else? Who he might be meetin' in Westport?"

"No, but Hannah said she had seen 'im before at Maud's house, but didn't know 'is last name. She mentioned he ran messages from Dublin to Westport for da Brotherhood."

"Ahhh! Brilliant Milly! Yar quite the undercover agent Milly! Ya fadher would be proud of ya!"

"Hannah told me dis fella often met members of da Brotherhood in Westport at a secret location, some place called the Reek? Ya ever hear of such a place?"

"The Reek!" exclaimed Scott. "Ah Milly, ya are da manna

from 'eaven, for sure lass! Oh… The Reek und I are most well-acquainted, Milly! Ya've done ya job beyond m' wildest imagination lass! Und dis is where we must now part! I promise ya, I'll be in touch, just as soon as I 'ave tracked down dis Mr. Joseph Fáinne!" Scott rose hastily, grabbed his suitcase, flung his coat over his arm and galloped out the hotel, leaving Milly slightly bewildered, and still gasping for breath.

Croagh Patrick, or the Reek as it was known by locals, stands at an elevation of just over 764 meters or 2506 feet and is a moderate to strenuous climb at times. It sits about 9.7 kilometres west of Westport. Someone in Scott's physical condition could climb to the summit in a little under three hours. The unknown question to Scott was how long would it take for Joe Fáinne to reach the summit? Fáinne was a good ten years younger than Scott and had clearly ascended Croagh Patrick many times delivering messages to his contact. The train for Westport had already left, so Scott had the disadvantage, he'd have to move fast once he reached the Reek to catch up, since the next train wouldn't leave for another hour.

In fine weather the ascent of Croagh Patrick would be challenging at times, particularly the final climb to the summit where the footing can be most treacherous. Scott knew this well. With less favourable weather conditions he also knew the climb would require greater caution. A fall during this final ascend could mean serious injury or certain death. As the train to Westport pulled into the station Scott could see the Reek looming in the distance, the mist swooping in fast around its peak. Cloud cover sat low today, and a fine, damp mist persisted hauntingly.

As Scott moved up the mountain trail, the mist began to engulf his mammoth profile. His boots trudging upward through the thickening mist now expanding to fog. At times, he thought he heard echoes of footsteps ahead of him and he stopped and cocked his ear upward to the summit to listen intently. He seemed to discern distant murmurs carried by the now dense fog filed air. As a child, he always thought Croagh Patrick alive; a living, sentient being, its rock groaning under the footsteps of the countless boots that have ascended its peak over the centuries. Now, Scott merely respected the Reek for its majestic presence. A constant reminder of nature's timeless justice, as he saw it. As the wind grew stronger and the fog appeared to become denser, Scott's boots struggled for a steady grip. The loose rock peeled away from the mountainside under Scott's hefty boots like layers of an onion. As he gradually made his way up the final path to the summit, the wind quickly changed direction and the sounds of muffled men's voices could be heard. Now breathing deeply, Scott rallied and moved more hastily toward his prey.

The white chapel built in 1905 crested the summit upon a craggy hill, clouds surrounding its whitewashed walls with Clew Bay now indistinct by the surrounding fog far below. The sounds of distant seagulls the only signal of the bay. He approached more stealthily now, his boots barely skimming the ground; a giant hawk hovering closer to the chapel sensing its prey at close quarters. The voices now grew clearer: two men in brief bursts of heated conversation. Scott drew his weapon and moved to the door to listen closer. An older man's voice spoke, punctuated by moments of silence, seemingly for dramatic effect. A younger man's voice interrupted from time to time and spoke more brashly than the older fellow. The young man appeared to become impatient at the responses given by his partner. Scott could only discern odd words here and there as the wind recklessly whipped around the chapel and accosted his face. The exchange between the two men tapered off, with greater pauses as the air outside appeared to become heavier. Footsteps could be heard moving toward the door inside the chapel and Scott slid to one side to remain concealed, his weapon still drawn and trained at the simple wooden door. An old man in his sixties emerged, dressed as a priest, followed steadily by a much younger suited, stouter fellow wearing some well-worn boots. Both men carried coats draped over their arms.

Scott waited patiently for the men to move beyond his position behind the great wooden door, and then took one giant leap forward.

"Good evenin' to ya, gentl'men!" announced Scott. The effect took both men by surprise as they swivelled to greet Scott's hulking shadow pointing his weapon squarely in their faces. "Ahhh, doncha worry, fellas, I'm widh da local police force. Da name's Detective Inspect'r William Scott. Pleased to meet ya both! 'Tis un interesting place for a meetin' doncha tink fellas?'

The men had not moved an inch, and stood like a pair of granite statues, appearing as though neither man were breathing. Finally, the priest broke the silence:

"Detective Inspect'r Scott, I recognize da name, pleased to meet ya too, I'm sure," the priest paused before continuing. "Tis a cold and damp night to be outsid' t'nite. Is dare som'sing we culd assist ya widh Detective?" queried the priest coyly.

"Ahhh, I'm happy ya asked, Fadher. May I ask wot ya gentl'men were doin' up 'ere so late on such an inhospitable night? Joe Fáinne's face started to turn sour, his eyes fixated upon Scott and his weapon. Scott noticed his sudden change in demeanour.

"Und who's dis fella widh ya Fadher?" Scott nodded in the young man's direction. The priest turned to introduce the young man.

"Dis is young Jimmy Flannigan, und he needed to meet me to discuss his upcoming nuptials widh his bride," continued the priest without hesitation.

"Ahhh… is dhat so Fadher? I see. Mister Flannigan, 'ave we met before? Coz, ya look familiar?" enquired Scott.

Fáinne now faced Scott; their eyes locked together in a stoical fashion.

"Nah, I cunnat say I've ever 'ad the pleasure, Detective Inspect'r." He moved to place his hands into his coat pocket, as he did so, Scott's eyes narrowed and trained his weapon closely upon Fáinne. The priest protested, feigning indignation at being accosted.

"Ya'll 'ave to excuse me Fadher, but deese are tryin' times, und an officer of da law cunnat be too karfle deese dahys, doncha know? Fadher, Mr. Flannigan, is it? Lemme escort ya down the Reek, if ya please?" Scott motioned to the two men to begin their descent. The priest nodded in compliance and Fáinne looking perturbed moved forward down the trail. The two men walked on, while Scott held back a few paces and followed; his weapon now down at his side.

"Do tell me Mr. Flannigan, who is dis lucky bride?"

"A young lass from Murrisk," responded the priest. Scott didn't seem impressed.

"Tank-ya Fadher, fur answering, but I woz askin' Mr. Flannigan 'ere." Fáinne still with his back to Scott turned slightly with a scowl noticeably upon his face.

"Ask me wot ya wont, Detective Inspect'r, I 'ave nothin' t' hide."

"I'm glad to hear dhat Mr. Flannigan. Dhen ya won't mind if ya follow me back t' Westport police station will ya?"

"Is dis entirely necessary, Detective Inspect'r? Interjected the priest.

"It's just procedure, Fadher," clarified Scott.

"So now the folks of Westport are bein' harassed by law enforcement?" snarled Fáinne.

"Call it wot ya may, Mr. Flannigan, m' job is to protect da local community, und dhat's wot I am sworn t' do."

Fáinne could hold out no longer, there was a sudden scuffle as he quickly turned, grabbing the priest's walking cane and swinging it wildly in Scott's direction to disarm him. The cane caught Scott's hand, and the pistol went flying five feet into the air before landing on some rocks and discharging a stray bullet. Fáinne now dove toward Scott, as the priest hurriedly dashed down the trail leaving the two men locked together in each other's grasp. Fáinne's eyes were now cold and soulless as Scott grappled with him, getting one paw firmly around Fáinne's left forearm; his giant hands appeared like eagle's talons wrapped around its prey. Muffled sounds came from both men, as they fought to secure a stronger hold over the other. Fáinne moved his hand to his waist, but seeing this Scott pushed him backward regaining some ground among the craggy rocks. He quickly removed a knife and pointed it toward Scott.

Scott regained his composure, shaking off the dust from his clothes. "Joseph Fáinne, I strongly suggest you put down dhat knife und com' widh me, yar under arrest lad!" yelled Scott.

Fáinne charged at Scott like a rabid, wild dog; a crazed look in his eye and with the knife held in a striking motion – swiped at him. But Scott was quick on his feet and jumped backward out of harm's way. Another quick second and Fáinne charged Scott again; this time he stumbled on loose rock but caught himself as Fáinne took another deadly strike at Scott's upper torso. The detective deflected the blow effortlessly with a kick and the knife went flying into some larger boulders. The two men were now unarmed, with fists raised. They moved further down the trail as they faced off; each man throwing a series of quick successive punches, some landing and some failing to hit their target. Scott still had the advantage of height over Fáinne and landed several blows to Fáinne's head and upper body. Fáinne stumbled a few times and lost his footing falling backward.

"I'd give it up Fáinne, com' widh me now; you're tired," roared Scott.

"I'll never give up, ya loyalist bastard; you'll 'ave to kill me!" barked Fáinne.

Fáinne energetically charged Scott again, as the detective lost his footing and fell backwards; his head narrowly missing some large boulders where the knife had landed. Within a second, Fáinne pounced on top, his fists striking Scott rapidly without mercy.

The knife sat within reach of Fáinne as he quickly searched for it while still grappling with Scott's enormous arms. The knife now in Fáinne's grasp he raised it to strike Scott in the chest. And as the knife began its trajectory downward, a sudden and deafening gunshot rang out from behind. Fáinne collapsed — blood poured from a large gaping back wound. Scott laid momentarily stunned before slowly pushing the lifeless body aside with a giant swipe. He looked up in the direction of the gunshot. Gasping for breath, he gradually regained his composure and stood.

"Milly! By gawd! He gathered himself, taking several deep breaths before continuing... "I tink... I tink..." Scott gasped for breath, "dhat I owe ya a great debt of gratitude. But how... did ya know where I woz?" Milly stood silent with the pistol still raised in her hands... a look of shear disbelief on her face... Scott staggered forward slightly before regaining his composure.

She lowered the pistol and took a deep sigh of relief. "A young lad by da name of Henry Desmond saw ya climbing the Reek. I bumped into 'im after I followed ya to Westport. I had a feelin' ya still needed m' help," she stuttered, still in shock.

Milly stood for several moments longer in complete silence. Scott stood motionless. "It's okay lass... it's okay, ya saved m' life! Dhat fella woz an evil, twisted brute... bound by nature to destroy anything he came across. It's okay lass..." Scott moved in closer to place a hand on her shoulder. "Jimmy would have been proud of ya, Milly. Ya saved many a life tonight."

Milly moved toward Scott to embrace him. The two stood silently for several moments before moving. Their silhouettes eventually vanishing as they traversed the rocky trail back down the mountain. The fog slowly enveloping them in the distance as Fáinne's body lay alone, face down among the inhospitable, precipitous rubble. As they vanished down the mountainside, his body now swallowed whole by the Reek's rugged landscape. Scott turned back momentarily and considered it befitting Fáinne lay consumed by Croagh Patrick.

"Wot now Mr. Scott?" Queried Milly.

"You cunh stay the night at m' house Milly. Our journey has only just begun. Tah-morrah, we take on the establishment."

Epilogue

Young *Maggie*, or Marjorie Milling, was my paternal grandmother. In her later years she lived in Northern Ireland, where as a child I recall many a laconic sojourn with her in the small and quaint coastal town of Helen's Bay. My first impressions of those encounters as a younger lad were of an austere matriarch who rarely smiled or showed any outward affection. As I matured and learned more about those horrific events surrounding her father's murder, I grew more empathetic. Marjorie was a woman carrying an overwhelming burden of sadness and deep-seated bitterness. I have no doubt she was close to her father and that he treated her well. Perhaps even, she was a Daddy's girl — at least that's what I would like to think.

The over-powering essence of terrorism is to create fear and mayhem, yet even through chaos and war we find the great collective spirit of humankind — our steadfast ability to come together and help our fellow humans in times of dire need. I witnessed first-hand in Marjorie the effects of the power of harbouring such great ill will. It will consume you, with every fibre of your being and you will wither away.

I am not condemning or passing judgement on my grandmother (God rest her soul), for I cannot imagine the unfathomable grief and pain of witnessing her father's murder, or the subsequent traumatic upheaval of her life and that of my great-grandmother's in the years that followed. These are the unseen, nameless victims of such crimes that have been mirrored around the world countless times. Nonetheless, when you fall victim yourself to hatred and disgust, nothing will ever grow from that barren field. She never spoke of the events of that fatal night, not even with my own father. In her later years, Marjorie succumbed to Alzheimer's in her early 80s and moved to Scotland to live with my aunt until she passed peacefully in her late 80s.

I have chosen to dedicate this novel to all those nameless victims who carry the burden of those who consciously and wilfully take life and terrorize others. I remind myself of an old Gaelic saying: *Ar scáth a chéile a mhaireann na daoine*[1] — Loosely translated, it means *people live in each other's shadows*. That seems to fit quite well here — we all live in the shadow of something that has come before us. And we all inherit some sense of affinity with the world around us from those who have preceded us, and more importantly — how we react to the world around us. Some take the easy path, while others choose to return something to humanity, however small. As time passes the names of those who terrorize eventually fade away into dust, but humanity will forever celebrate the names of its greatest artists, writers, politicians, scientists, inventors, and humanitarians throughout the generations. In the end, we all have a choice: to create or destroy. The legacy will always be ours to make and to pass along.

Chapter One

[1] Fenian Rising: The Fenian Rising of 1867 was a rebellion against British rule in Ireland, organized by the Irish Republican Brotherhood (IRB).

[2] Home Rule Bill: The term "Home Rule", was first introduced in the 1860s, and essentially meant an Irish legislature with responsibility for domestic affairs. To nationalists, it was viewed as nothing more than a part of a federal system for the United Kingdom (domestic Parliament for Ireland while the Imperial Parliament at Westminster would continue to have responsibility for Imperial affairs). The Republican concept as represented by the Fenians and the Irish Republican Brotherhood, strove to achieve total separation from Great Britain, by any means necessary, and succeed in bringing about total autonomy for Ireland.

Chapter Two

[1] Plymouth brethren: The Plymouth Brethren are a conservative, low church, nonconformist, Evangelical Christian movement whose history can be traced to Dublin, Ireland in the late 1820s, originating from Anglicanism. Among other beliefs, the group emphasizes sola scriptura, the belief that the Bible is the supreme authority for church doctrine and practice over and above "the [mere] tradition of men" (Mark 7:8). Brethren generally see themselves not as a denomination but as a network, or even as a collection of overlapping networks, of like-minded independent churches.

[2] Phoenix Park Training Depot: Phoenix Park Training Depot: The Royal Irish Constabulary's police training barracks from 1822–1922. In 1922, the RIC was disbanded, and the barracks was turned over to the Garda Siochana (Guardians of the Peace) — Ireland's newly established police force in the Republic of Ireland.

[3] Sinn Fein: Sinn Féin (pronounced shin-fayn), is an Irish republican political party active in the Republic of Ireland and Northern Ireland. The name is Irish for "ourselves" or "we ourselves", although it is frequently mistranslated as "ourselves alone". The Sinn Féin organization was founded in 1905 by Arthur Griffith. It took its current form in 1970 after a split within the party (the other party became the Workers' Party of Ireland), and has been historically associated with the Provisional Irish Republican Army (IRA). Gerry Adams has been party president since 1983.

Chapter Three

[1] Croagh Patrick: Croagh Patrick (Irish: Cruach Phádraig, meaning "(Saint) Patrick's Stack"), nicknamed the Reek, is a 764 metre (2,507 ft) mountain and an important site of pilgrimage in County Mayo in Ireland. It is eight kilometres (five miles) from Westport, above the villages of Murrisk and Lecanvey. The third highest mountain in County Mayo after Mweelrea and Nephin, Croagh Patrick is climbed by pilgrims on Reek Sunday every year, which is the last Sunday in July. It forms the southernmost part of a U-shaped valley created by a glacier flowing into Clew Bay in the last Ice Age. Croagh Patrick is part of a longer east-west ridge; the westernmost peak is called Ben Gorm.

[2] John MacBride: 7 May 1868 – 5 May 1916, an Irish Republican and military leader who was executed by the British for his part in the Easter Rising of 1916 in Dublin. He fought in the Second Boer War against the British, where he raised the Irish Transvaal Brigade. MacBride was commissioned with the rank of major in the Boer army and given Boer citizenship. After the Second Boer War he travelled to Paris where he met Maud Gonne. In 1905 John MacBride married Maud Gonne to many protestations from W.B. Yeats.

[3] Second Boer War: or "Second Freedom War", usually known as the Boer War, began on 11 October 1899 and ended on 31 May 1902. Great Britain defeated two Boer states in South Africa: the South African Republic

(Republic of Transvaal) and the Orange Free State. Britain was aided by its Cape Colony, Colony of Natal and some native African allies. The British war effort was further supported by volunteers from the British Empire, including South Africa, the Australian colonies, Canada, India, and New Zealand. All other nations were neutral, but public opinion in them was largely hostile toward Britain. Inside Britain and its Empire there also was significant opposition to the Second Boer War.

[4] Maud Gonne : Maud Gonne MacBride (21 December, 1866 – 27 April, 1953) was an English-born Irish revolutionary, suffragette and actress. Maud was of Anglo-Irish descent, and took up the cause of Irish nationalism through the struggles of evicted people in the Land Wars. Maud also actively supported for Home Rule (the power of an administrative division, in this case Ireland, to exercise the state's powers of governance within its own administrative area). Maud was also a close friend and confidant to W.B. Yeats, to whose affections she toyed with and subsequently refused four marriage proposals. Yeats considered her his muse, and Maud believed that marrying him would be an utter disservice to Yeats, citing his unrequited love and angst as inspiration for his work. Yet, it is reported that they finally consummated their relationship in Paris in 1908; but even this failed to solidify acceptance on Maud's end of marriage. Yeats himself casually wrote: "*the tragedy of sexual intercourse is the perpetual virginity of the soul.*"

[5] Arthur Griffith (31 March 1872 – 12 August 1922) was an Irish politician and writer, who founded and later led the political party Sinn Féin. He served as President of Dáil Éireann from January to August 1922 and was head of the Irish delegation at the negotiations in London that produced the Anglo-Irish Treaty of 1921, attending with Michael Collins.

[6] Easter Rising of 1916: The Easter Rising, also known as the Easter Rebellion, was an armed insurrection in Ireland that began on Easter

Monday, 24 April 1916 and continued through Easter week. The Rising was launched by Irish republicans (members of the Irish Republican Brotherhood) to end British rule in Ireland and establish an independent Irish Republic as the United Kingdom was heavily engaged in World War I. The Easter Rising was the most significant uprising in Ireland since the rebellion of 1798.

[7] Thomas MacDonagh: (1 February 1878 – 3 May 1916) was an Irish political activist, poet, playwright, educationalist and revolutionary leader. He was one of the seven leaders of the Easter Rising of 1916, a signatory of the Proclamation of the Irish Republic and Commandant of the 2nd Battalion, Dublin Brigade of the Irish Volunteers, which fought in Jacob's biscuit factory. He was executed for his part in the Rising at the age of thirty-eight at Kilmainham Gaol. MacDonagh was assistant headmaster at St. Enda's School, Scoil Éanna, and lecturer in English at University College Dublin. He was a member of the Gaelic League, where he befriended Patrick Pearse and Eoin MacNeill. He was a founding member of the Irish Volunteers with MacNeill and Pearse. He wrote poetry and plays.

[8] Jacob's Biscuit Factory: The biscuit making firm of W. & R. Jacob's was one the largest employers in the Dublin of 1916. The factory was seized on Easter Monday by approximately 100 members of the 2nd Battalion of the Dublin Brigade of the Irish Volunteers, led by Thomas MacDonagh. The factory itself was an enormous and formidable Victorian edifice located on the 'block' enclosed by Bishop St, Bride St, Peter's St and Peter's Row, and between St Patrick's Cathedral and St Stephen's Green. Its seizure helped to complete a loop of buildings crossing the south inner city. The factory had two large towers that provided suitable observation points, while its location was very close to both Camden Street and Patrick Street: as it turns out, natural routes for troops entering the city centre from the Portobello Barracks in Rathmines and Wellington Barracks on the South Circular Road.

Chapter Five
[1] Castlebar: (Irish: Caisleán an Bharraigh, meaning "Barry's Castle") is the county town of County Mayo, Ireland. Castlebar is positioned in the middle of the county and is its largest town by population. The modern town grew up as a settlement around the de Barry castle, and was built by the Normans in 1235. The castle later became the site of an English garrison. Castlebar Military Barracks operated in the town for many years and eventually closed in March 2012. Armed conflict has been the centrepiece of the town's historical heritage for centuries.

[2] D&SER: D&SER – The Dublin and South Eastern Railway (D&SER) was originally incorporated, by Act of Parliament in 1846, as the *Waterford, Wexford, Wicklow and Dublin Railway Company*; incorporated 1846, the first section opened 1856.

Chapter Six
[1] Castlebar: (Irish: Caisleán an Bharraigh, meaning "Barry's Castle") is the county town of County Mayo, Ireland. Castlebar is positioned in the middle of the county and is its largest town by population. The modern town grew up as a settlement around the de Barry castle, and was built by the Normans in 1235. The castle later became the site of an English garrison. Castlebar Military Barracks operated in the town for many years and eventually closed in March 2012. Armed conflict has been the centrepiece of the town's historical heritage for centuries. Phoenix Park Training Depot[2]: Phoenix Park Training Depot was the training college for all Royal Irish Constabulary (RIC) recruits, until the declaration of the Irish Free State in 1922. Following the newly created Irish Free State, the RIC was disbanded and replaced by the Garda Síochána (Gaelic translation: Guardians of the Peace).

The ruins of an RIC barracks at Deergrove, Islandeady, still stands as testimony to the reminder of a troubled past in Ireland. These barracks comprise just one of sixty-three barracks and police huts scattered across

County Mayo where over four hundred men were deployed during the nineteenth and early twentieth centuries. In the 1920s, during a period of particularly violent unrest in the country, the authorities vacated many rural barracks and evacuated the police to the relative safety of the larger centres. The force at Islandeady was transferred to the surrounding towns and the barrack was left undefended. On Easter Sunday night, 1920, the building was set alight by "persons unknown" and considerable damage was done. The 'Connaught Telegraph' of 12 June 1920, reported that a malicious damage claim for one thousand pounds was lodged in a Castlebar court.

The RIC was the first countrywide police force formed in 1822 and was known as the Irish Constabulary. On 6 September 1867, Queen Victoria, recognising its 'loyal and faithful service' in the suppression of the uprising by the Irish Republican Brotherhood, honoured the IC with the title "Royal". She decreed that 'henceforth' the Force was to wear the Crown and Shamrock insignia on their uniforms. The duties of the RIC were varied; apart from normal policing, they included gathering intelligence, checking the sale of food and drink, estimating the size of the potato crop, maintaining order at elections, preventing wakes for those people who had died of infectious diseases, to name a few. Many RIC officers were killed in the line of duty.

The RIC were disbanded in 1922 when the border with Northern Ireland was imposed. The RIC in the north became known as the RUC (Royal Ulster Constabulary) and in the south, the force became the Garda Siochana (Guardians of the Peace).

[2] Arthur Griffith: (31 March 1872 – 12 August 1922) was an Irish politician and writer, who founded and later led the political party, Sinn Féin. He served as President of Dáil Éireann from January to August 1922 and was head of the Irish delegation at the negotiations in London that produced the Anglo-Irish Treaty of 1921, attending with Michael Collins.

[3] Francis Sheehy-Skeffington: During the Easter Rising, Sheehy-

Skeffington, who had been living at 11 (now 21), Grosvenor Place, Rathmines, Dublin, was concerned about the collapse of law and order. On the evening of Tuesday, 25 April, he went into the city centre to attempt to organize a citizens' militia to prevent the looting of local businesses. He was arrested for no stated, or indeed obvious, reason while returning home, by members of the 11th East Surrey Regiment at Portobello Bridge along with some hecklers who were following him, and, after admitting to having sympathy for the insurgents' cause (but not their tactics), he was held as an enemy sympathizer. Later that evening, an officer of the 3rd battalion Royal Irish Rifles, Captain JC Bowen-Colthurst sent Sheehy-Skeffington out with an army raiding party in Rathmines, held as a hostage with his hands tied behind his back. The raiding party were ordered by Bowen-Colthurst that he was to be shot if it was attacked. He went to the home and shop of Alderman James Kelly at the corner of Camden Street and Harcourt Road, from which the name "Kelly's Corner" derives. Mistaking the Alderman (who was a Conservative) for Alderman Tom Kelly, the soldiers destroyed the shop with hand grenades. Bowen-Colthurst took captive a young boy, and two pro-British journalists who were in the shop — Thomas Dickson and Patrick MacIntyre — and a Labour Party politician, Richard O'Carroll. He shot O'Carroll in the lungs and shot the boy as he knelt to pray. Skeffington witnessed and protested at the murders of the boy and O'Carroll on the way through Rathmines. Bowen-Colthurst told him: "You'll be next". The two journalists and Sheehy-Skeffington were taken out to a yard in the barracks and shot by an ad hoc firing squad on Bowen-Colthurst's orders the following morning.

[4] Fenian rising: The Fenian Rising of 1867, was a rebellion against British rule in Ireland, organised by the Irish Republican Brotherhood (IRB).

Chapter Eight

[1] Kilmainham Jail: (Gaol) was a former prison in Kilmainham, Dublin, Ireland. It's now a museum run by the Office of Public Works, an agency of

the Government of Ireland. Many Irish revolutionaries, including the leaders of the 1916 Easter Rising, were imprisoned and executed in the prison by the British.

[2] Easter Rising of 1916: The Easter Rising, also known as the Easter Rebellion, was an armed insurrection in Ireland that began on Easter Monday, 24 April 1916 and continued through Easter week. The Rising was launched by Irish republicans (members of the Irish Republican Brotherhood) to end British rule in Ireland and establish an independent Irish Republic as the United Kingdom was heavily engaged in World War I. The Easter Rising was the most significant uprising in Ireland since the rebellion of 1798.

[3] Eamon De Valera: Eamon Da Valera, 3rd President of Ireland. He was born 14 October 1882 and died on 29 August 1975. Da Valera served as president of Ireland from 25 June 1959 to 24 June 1973. Although Da Valera distanced himself from the call for a show of physical force against British rule in Ireland, it is debatable whether Da Valera's words were merely rhetoric coming from a man with higher reaching political aspirations.

[4] John Devoy: 1842 – 29 September 1928, was an Irish rebel leader living in exile. Devoy was owner and editor of the Gaelic American, a New York weekly newspaper, 1903 – 1928. Devoy dedicated over sixty years of his life to the cause of Irish freedom. He is one of the few people to have played a leading role in the rebellion of 1867, the 1916 Easter Rising and the Irish War of Independence (1919 – 1921).

[5] Michael Collins: 16 October 1890 – 22 August 1922, was an Irish revolutionary leader, politician, Minister for Finance, Director of Information, and Teachta Dála (TD) for Cork South in the First Dáil of 1919. Adjutant General, Director of Intelligence, and Director of Organisation and Arms Procurement for the IRA, President of the Irish Republican

Brotherhood from November 1920 until his death, and member of the Irish delegation during the Anglo-Irish Treaty negotiations. Subsequently, he was both Chairman of the Provisional Government and Commander-in-chief of the National Army. Collins was shot and killed in an ambush in August 1922 during the Irish Civil War.

[6] Clan na Gael: is an Irish republican organization in the United States in the late 19th and 20th centuries, successor to the Fenian Brotherhood and a sister organization to the Irish Republican Brotherhood. It has shrunk to a small fraction of its former size in the 21st century.

[7] Café Cairo: The Cairo Gang was a group of British intelligence agents who were sent to Dublin during the Irish War of Independence to conduct intelligence operations against prominent members of the Irish Republican Army (IRA) — according to Irish intelligence, with the intention of assassinating them. Twelve men including British Army officers, Royal Irish Constabulary officers and a civilian informant, were killed on the morning of 21 November 1920 by the Irish Republican Army in a planned series of simultaneous early-morning strikes engineered by Michael Collins. The events were to be the first killings of Bloody Sunday. It has been suggested that the Cairo Gang's nom de guerre came from their choice of frequent meetings held at Café Cairo at 59 Grafton Street in Dublin.

Chapter Nine

[1] Milling Tax: Lilla Milling, John Charles Milling's spouse, was awarded 6,000 pounds including full costs, with two-fifths assessed on the rates of Westport UDC, and another two-fifths on County of Mayo. The county council appealed this, and a subsequent ruling placed the whole burden on Westport. In August, the Mayo News had dubbed this levy as the Milling Tax.

[2] Marchioness of Sligo and Lord Altamont: The Marchioness and Lord Altamont attended John Charles Milling's funeral, where it is assumed he was buried with his sister.

[3] Gunshots rang out in the Milling home: On the night of Sunday 29 March 1919, John C. Milling was shot and fatally wounded while at home in Westport. The following account of that night is referenced from Penny Bonsall's *The Irish RM's: Resident Magistrates in the British Administration in Ireland*, published by Four Courts Press: At approximately 11 o'clock, John Milling left the dining room crossing the hall to move into the drawing room, where he planned to wind the clock and adjust it to British summer time. The curtains were drawn back, the blind was up, and the room illuminated only by a lamp he was carrying. Shots then rang out, fired through the window of the drawing room and striking the RM in the shoulder and abdomen. He staggered back through the hall to the dining room, but at that time more shots were fired through the window, one of them barely missing Lilla Milling. James Sheridan, who lived next door to the Millings heard shots, and upon seeing no one outside went over to knock at the Milling's door. The RM answered the door, bleeding profusely and informed Sheridan he had been shot. Lilla had briefly fainted, but soon revived and she and Sheridan helped the RM upstairs to his bed and made him comfortable. DI Scott who lodged with the Sheridan's was soon on the scene and checking the rooms for evidence. Two doctors attended the RM. The Castle was informed, and specialist medical help was promptly dispatched overnight from Dublin. John Milling was a robust man in excellent health, and he lingered on in great pain until 10 o'clock the following night when he finally succumbed to his wounds. As he lay dying, he said: 'they've got me at last.' His final request was that his wife should be looked after. He reportedly told the attending doctor that he had repeatedly asked for a transfer, 'but they would not grant it, and this was the result.'

Chapter Ten

[1] D&SER: D&SER – The Dublin and South Eastern Railway (D&SER) was originally incorporated, by Act of Parliament in 1846, as the *Waterford, Wexford, Wicklow and Dublin Railway Company*; incorporated 1846, the first section opened 1856.

[2] Gresham Hotel: The Gresham Hotel, named after its founder, Thomas Gresham, was opened in 1817 and is a four-star hotel on O'Connell Street in Dublin, Ireland. It is a Dublin institution and landmark building and was badly damaged during the Irish Civil War but rebuilt during the 1920s.

[3] Meejum of Guinness: John McHale's pub on Chapel Street Lower in Castlebar. Made famous for serving a "meejum" of Guinness. Rather than a half or a pint, you get a measure somewhere in between.

[4] Captain McCormack: Captain Patrick McCormack and Lieutenant Leonard Wilde were staying at the Gresham Hotel in O'Connell Street. The IRA unit gained access to their rooms by pretending to be British soldiers with important dispatches. When the men opened their doors, they were shot and killed. A Times listing for McCormack and Wilde does not list any rank for the latter. McCormack's killing was a mistake. He was a member of the Royal Army Veterinary Corps and was in Ireland to buy horses for the British Army. He was shot in bed and Collins himself later acknowledged the error. Unlike the other British officers, McCormack, a Catholic from Castlebar, was buried in Ireland, at Glasnevin Cemetery, Dublin.

[5] Leonard Aidan Wilde: joined the army as an officer when he was an ecclesiastical student. He suffered from shell shock in July 1916 and was invalided out of the army. He then joined the Foreign Office as a Consular Official in Spain. James Doyle, the Gresham Hotel Manager, seemed confident that the suspiciously named Wilde was indeed a spy, having been told that Wilde was thrown out of Spain because he was well known there to be a British agent. (www.cairogang.com)

[6] The Marrowbone Lane Distillery: was an Irish whiskey distillery located on Marrowbone Lane, in Dublin, Ireland. Synonymous as one of the big four historical Dublin whiskey makers. Run by William Jameson, a member of

the Jameson whiskey dynasty. The same whiskey now known as Jameson Irish Whiskey was not produced at this distillery, but at a separate facility run by John Jameson, nearby at Bow Street Distillery. In 1923 the distillery closed due to financial difficulties.

[7] Bloody Sunday: Bloody Sunday was a day of violence in Dublin on 21 November 1920, during the Irish War of Independence. A total of thirty-one people were killed; including fourteen British agents and RIC personnel, fourteen Irish civilians, and three Irish republican prisoners. The Irish Republican Army (IRA) operation organized by Michael Collins was tasked with the assassination of members of the 'Cairo Gang' — a team of undercover British intelligence agents working and living in Dublin.

Chapter Eleven
[1] Croagh Patrick: Croagh Patrick (Irish: Cruach Phádraig, meaning "(Saint) Patrick's Stack"), nicknamed the Reek, is a 764 metre (2,507 ft) mountain and an important site of pilgrimage in County Mayo in Ireland. It is eight kilometres (five miles) from Westport, above the villages of Murrisk and Lecanvey. It is the third highest mountain in County Mayo after Mweelrea and Nephin. It is climbed by pilgrims on Reek Sunday every year, which is the last Sunday in July. It forms the southern part of a U-shaped valley created by a glacier flowing into Clew Bay in the last Ice Age. Croagh Patrick is part of a longer east-west ridge; the westernmost peak is called Ben Gorm.

[2] Ross & Co.: Ross and Co. of Dublin renown as one of the most important makers of campaign furniture in the Victorian era and still considered a leader in their field, today.

Eleanor Ross founded the company E. Ross at 6 Ellis Quay at the end of the 18th century. The business capitalized on the demand for portable furniture that accompanied the expansion of the British Empire in the 19th century.

Chapter Fourteen

[1] Meejum of Guinness: Jonny McHale's Pub, one of the oldest in Castelbar, still stands today. A public house where you can order a meejum (medium) of Guinness, rather than a half or a pint; you get a measure somewhere in between that. McHale's was once hailed by national tabloids as serving one of the best pints of Guinness in Ireland.

Chapter Seventeen

[1] *Ar dheas Dé go raibh a anam:* May his soul be at God's right hand.

[2] Maith thú!: Good on you!

Chapter Eighteen

[1] Hannah Moynihan: On 10 April 1923, Maud Gonne MacBride was arrested and charged by the authorities for painting banners for seditious demonstrations and preparing anti-government literature. According to the diary account of her colleague Hannah Moynihan: *"Last night [10th April] at 11pm, we heard the commotion which usually accompanies the arrival of new prisoners... we pestered the wardress and she told us there were four — Maud Gonne MacBride, her daughter Mrs. Iseult Stuart and two lesser lights... Early this morning... we could see Maud walking majestically past our cell door leading on a leash a funny little lap dog which answered to the name that sounded like Wuzzo."*

[2] St. Stephen's Green: On the death of Prince Albert, Queen Victoria suggested that St. Stephen's Green be renamed Albert Green and a statue of Albert be placed at its centre. This suggestion was rejected with indignation by the Dublin Corporation and the people of the city, much to Queen Victoria's displeasure. Access to the Green was restricted to local residents, until 1877, when Parliament passed an Act to reopen St. Stephen's Green to the public, at the initiative of Sir A.E. Guinness (member of the Guinness

brewing family). He later paid for the laying out of the Green in approximately its current form, which took place in 1880, and gave it to the Corporation, as representatives of the people. In recognition of his act of kindness, the city commissioned a statue of Guinness, which faces the College of Surgeons.

During the Easter Rising of 1916, a group of insurgents made up mainly of members of the Irish Citizen Army established a position in St Stephen's Green. They numbered between 200 and 250. Commandeering motor vehicles to establish road blocks on the streets that surround the park they dug defensive positions in the park itself. This approach proved unwise when the British Army took up positions in the Shelbourne Hotel, at the north-eastern corner of St Stephen's Green, overlooking the park, from which they could shoot down into the entrenchments. Finding themselves in a weak position, the Volunteers withdrew to the Royal College of Surgeons on the west side of the Green. During the Easter Rising, hostilities were temporarily halted to allow the park's grounds men to feed the local ducks.

[3] Nassau Street: Maud lived in rooms on Nassau Street where she reportedly presided over meetings with groups of young nationalists.

[4] Black and Tans: The Black and Tans established in 1919, were officially the Royal Irish Constabulary Special Reserve. A force of temporary constables recruited to assist the Royal Irish Constabulary during the Irish War of Independence. The force was the brainchild of Winston Churchill, then British Secretary of State for War.

[5] Johnnie Fox's Pub: Established in 1798 and noted as one of Dublin's oldest pubs. Johnnie Fox's has been at the center of Glencullen village since 1798, the year the Irish Rebellion was led by Wolfe Tone. It was also used for meetings by leaders during 1916 Easter Rising. Fox's boasts of being the highest pub in Dublin with amazing views of the city below. The pub is about 35 minutes south from the city center, but it is worth making the trek

for the atmosphere, traditional music, dancing, storytelling sessions and other entertainment seven nights a week.

[6] Andy Cooney[6]: Member of the Third Battalion of the Dublin Brigade and a suspected participant in the execution of the Cairo Gang. The Cairo Gang (nicknamed so, because they reportedly met at Café Cairo in Dublin) were a group of British intelligence agents who were sent to Dublin during the Irish War of Independence to conduct intelligence operations against prominent members of the Irish Republican Army (IRA). According to Irish intelligence the so-called Cairo Gang intended to assassinate prominent IRA members. Twelve men including British Army officers, Royal Irish Constabulary officers and a civilian informant were killed on the morning of 21 November 1920 by the Irish Republican Army in a planned series of simultaneous early-morning assassinations carried out by Michael Collins' death squad. The events were the first killings of the now notorious Bloody Sunday of 1920.

[7] Déan deifir: In Gaelic — Hurry up, literally meaning "make haste".

Chapter Twenty-One

[1] John Devoy: 3 September 1842 – 29 September 1928 was an Irish rebel leader and exile. He owned and edited the Gaelic American, a New York weekly newspaper, 1903–1928. Devoy dedicated over 60 years of his life to the cause of Irish independence. He was one of the few people to have played a role in the rebellion of 1867, the 1916 Rising and the Irish War of Independence (1919 – 1921). Devoy died on September 29, 1928, aged 86 from natural causes while visiting Atlantic City, New Jersey. His death was met with widespread mourning and his body was returned to Ireland where a state funeral was held. He was buried in Glasnevin Cemetery in June 1929. On 25 October 2016, a statue of Devoy was unveiled in Poplar Square, Naas, County Kildare.

[2] Fenian: A term applied to the Fenian Brotherhood and the Irish Republican Brotherhood — fraternal organisations dedicated to the establishment of an independent Irish Republic in the 19th and early 20th centuries.

Epilogue

[1] *Ar scáth a chéile a mhaireann na daoine*: Under the shelter of each other, people survive.

Lightning Source UK Ltd.
Milton Keynes UK
UKHW010633050722
405403UK00001B/190